ENTICED BY A REAL HITTA 2

L. RENEE

Enticed by A Real Hitta 2

PREVIOUSLY IN ENTICED BY A REAL HITTA 2

Kilo

No one had yet to see Louve, and I was sick of the lies that Tori was telling for her nappy-headed ass bestie. I could hear her ass now talking, and the more I thought about her and the little things I loved, I was missing her more but getting more pissed each day. The girls were missing their mother, and she was always calling them when I was not around, how convenient, not to mention KJ was Face Timing her daily but acting like he wasn't. Mrs. Lolly was a godsend and had spoken to Louve and switched up on my ass when Louve told her why she left. Now every time I go out, Mrs. Lolly always got a smart-ass comment with her old gray hair ass.

Like now I know she about to give my ass an ear full. I left early this morning and went to check on some business at the restaurant Drip and I was working on opening. I walked in, and her ass is right up on the couch, waiting for me as I expected. She looked me up and down and rolled her eyes.

"Is that side part of yours the reason for your early departure out this house?" she asked.

I laughed so hard because she was trying to say sidepiece and said side part. She ain't find shit funny though because she jumped up and was in my face quick as hell.

"Calm down Mrs. Lolly. I'm behaving myself, trust me. I was just out handling some business for the restaurant," I replied.

"Yea, well yo behind gone lose that good woman you got. Keep chasing behind them tots!" she spat as she pointed her finger in my face.

I was trying not to laugh, but she was in here trying to sound like Louve with the word she was using but was getting them wrong. Louve had been all in Mrs. Lolly's ear about me, giving her a bad impression of me.

"Its thots, not tots, and no ma'am, I am not chasing no one, but I am on the hunt to find my woman and bring her home where she belongs," I stated and hugged Mrs. Lolly before heading upstairs.

I had to bring my baby home. I missed her ass. I was trying to be patient like Mrs. Lolly advised me after she followed me around the house schooling me as she says. She told me Louve missed and loved me, but had to take this time for herself. She broke it down to me and let me know how Louve had taken care of people her whole adult life but has been spoiled by all the men around her without having her mother when she needed her the most. Louve was doing some much-needed soul searching to find herself. I completely understood because it was for the better, and she needed that growth. I understood loud and clear, I was dead ass wrong for the shit I did, and if Louve would just talk to me and come home, she would see that I was sorry and would do whatever I needed to prove it to her.

After Mrs. Lolly left me to my thoughts, I decided that I had enough of waiting to at least see her, so I called up my PI and had him do some research on Louve. I also gave him Mrs. Lolly info, so in case she was secretly meeting up with Louve, he could get the address from her. I needed to go ahead, purchase Louve a ring, and stop dragging my feet. I called up the jeweler and made an appointment to discuss designing a ring. From there, I handled a few things that I needed to with the business and made my way to let Naomi down face to face.

She had been blowing my phone up for days on in, and it was time to break it to her that this little fling was done.

———

"Yo, Naomi, don't even try to play that game with me ma cause you won't win!" I spat pissed off at the bullshit she was talking.

"Listen, Kilo. I don't know how it happened, but I ain't been with no one but you, and you can be pissed, but I'm keeping my baby," she replied, rolling her eyes and snapping her neck like a damn bird.

"NO, THE HELL YOU NOT!" I shouted and rushed her into the wall snatching her up by the neck.

"OWWW, you're hurting me!" she yelled out, clawing at my arms.

"GET A FUCKING ABORTION, OR SWIM WITH THE FISHES, BUT EITHER WAY YO ASS AIN'T KEEPING SHIT!" I shouted as I shoved her into the wall a little harder before letting her go.

Naomi dropped to the floor and started sobbing uncontrollably. She then started to scream and yell that I would pay for the shit I did to her. I had to bounce before I killed this dumb ass girl. I shook my head at her pathetic ass as I headed out the door. I needed a few drinks to get my mind right. The shit I had got myself into was too damn much, so I headed to the bar to drink this shit off.

———

I was feeling all the shots I threw back, and I knew I needed to get my ass home and in the bed. I left a blue face on the bar and attempted to get up, but the dizziness knocked back down into the barstool. I rubbed my eyes to focus my vision, and then I got up slower this time and made my way to the door. I walked out into the parking lot, and I felt like someone was watching me, but I brushed it off as the liquor. I let the cool breeze sober me up before I got in my car. When I started to feel less dizzy, I hopped in my car and started it up. I still felt that feeling as if someone had eyes on me, and I scanned my surroundings, but nothing seemed out of the ordinary.

I pulled off out the parking space and out the lot heading home to shower and eat. I had a text come in from Louve as I was at the light waiting, and I smiled wide as I read her message.

Louve Baby: I'll be coming to the house tomorrow, and I think we need to talk about everything. I love you and miss you Kilo, and you can stop texting me threatening messages. See you tomorrow. XOXO

I reread it and laughed because I had been threatening her ass. I wanted to hear her voice, but I didn't want to push my luck. The light changed, and I pulled off and started my text back to her.

POP! POP! POP! POP!

Gunshots rang out around me, and I swerved over, trying to dodge them as they kept coming at my car. I hopped on the highway and realized too late. I was heading in the wrong direction into oncoming traffic when another car swerved over, but we still collided sending my car in the air. All I could do was brace for the impact and pray to the Lord to forgive me for my sins before I came to meet him.

SKKKKRRRRTTTTT! BOOOOOOOMMMMM!

Louve

I finished that book and was on to another one but couldn't focus on my book because I kept getting calls from an unknown number, so I stepped outside my mother's room to take the call.

"Hello, I'm looking for the next of kin to a Mr. Kilondre Jones," the caller stated.

"Yes, this is Louve Luxe," I replied nervously.

"We need you to get to the trauma unit of Cedars Sinai Hospital immediately," she explained with urgency.

I hung and headed to the nurse station with tears streaming down my face. I was already at the hospital, and I wanted to tell them where I was headed, but I'd be back for my mom. I took the elevator down with my mind racing. I said a prayer for Kilo, and I prayed for the strength to deal with this.

I got down to the trauma and emergency unit, and they gave me the rundown of what happened and what to expect. Kilo was in emergency surgery and needed a blood transfusion. His car was shot up, and he went the wrong way on the highway and was in an accident. He was hit in the back by two bullets and had a bad head injury and a punctured lung from the crash.

I took the test immediately to see if I was a match. I had group texted everyone, and they were all in the waiting area waiting on me to come back out. Mrs. Lolly even came with the kids and prayed with us and over us. I was on pins and needles as I sat and waited. I couldn't believe this was happening. My ass was away all this time, and this is what I come back to.

Edge was pacing back and forth, and I made Tori keep her eye on him because I knew he would try to go out and do some stupid, reckless ass shit that we didn't need. Tori was a mess and tried to hold it together for me, but we were all a family, so it was hard on us all. We were all we had. Drip was losing it. He couldn't reach Egypt, and that had him tripping hard. He was waiting on the word about Kilo, but I told him to find Egypt and check on her because none of us had heard from her at all today. I was worried about everyone right about now because it's no telling what the hell these guys have been out here doing to have this type shit happen.

I pleaded with Drip, and he went to look for Egypt just as the doctors came back and told me I wasn't a match. Everyone lined up to try to be a match, and that warmed my hurting heart. As time passed on, they said each of us wasn't a match, and we were running out of crucial time. I had no clue what we were going to do, but Mrs. Lolly stood up and offered to try.

"I believe I may be a match because Kilondre is my paternal grandson," she said, letting tears drop as her lip quivered.

"What are you saying? Mrs. Lolly, what is going on?" I said in disbelief.

"I had been conducting some research to verify, and when I took my son, who is a mental facility, a picture of Kilondre, he said that was his son. See, Kilondre's mother went to jail for killing my son's wife. They were in a love triangle gone wrong. My son Killon Denton was a big man out in the streets in the early '80s, and he had women all over him, but his wife Tracy was his boss' daughter. That's why he married her and was in love with Kilondre's mother, Kima. Tracy tried to kill Killon for attempting to leave her for Kilondre's mother and his son. Kima saved Killon's life by killing Tracy before she could kill him.

Kima went to jail for this, and Tracy's father made sure she got long hard time from his connections in the system. Killon was told that Kima was killed in jail, and he lost his mind. All this time, we were told Tracy's family killed Kilondre. However, when I came to interview for the nanny position and seen Kilo, I knew he was my grandson. I didn't know how to tell him and was waiting for the right time. However, if I am a match and can save my grandson's life, then I had to let it be known," she said sobbing.

I was at a loss for words and just grabbed her and hugged her tightly. They led her back to see if she was a match, and we all sat and waited again. I needed to tell Edge about our mother but now wasn't the time. I would wait until they had settled everything, and Kilo was in recovery because my baby was gone pull through. I had faith. No matter how hard it was, I had to keep the faith. I held my babies as well waited, and I rubbed my belly for the one growing in there. Our family wasn't complete without Kilo, and I wanted no life without my soul mate.

Drip

I had called Egypt and left so many voicemails that her mailbox was now full. I know she was mad as hell at me, but right now was important, and I needed to know that she was ok. I know she thought that I was out here doing her dirty, but I wasn't. I was tied up with *that shit we had to do with Saga and getting shit cleared up with the Dons. I went to our house, and her car wasn't there, and then I remembered that I put the GPS tracker on her car, so I logged in and pressed the locate button. I plugged the location in my car and was on my way to wherever she was.*

I was far as hell out the way of where we live damn near in Hollywood. I pulled up to the address, and it was nice ass townhome. I sat and contemplated a few possible scenarios, and the best way I should react and handle this shit. I was cool as hell and about to just ring the bell and see what was up because it could be a coworker's home and not no nigga like my mind was yelling at me that it was.

I parked right in front of the driveway blocking her car in because if it was some foul shit, I know how Egypt gets. She tries to run off, but not today. I was almost out the driveway when I doubled back to the car, the same car I saw her ass get out of in front of that restaurant with that nigga Pras before. I walked around the car to check the license plate praying with each step it wouldn't be the plate — however, no such luck. The Lord had been stopped answering my prayers with my fucked-up ass ways. I ain't surprised. It was that nigga Pras' car as expected.

I stormed to the door and started beating that bitch down. It took about five minutes before anyone came to the door. That nigga peeped out the window blinds, we made eye contact, and then I assumed he walked away. He never opened the door, and that pissed me off more, so I started kicking that shit trying to break it in. I jumped off the porch and ran to my car to get my gun. I was done playing nice with this nigga, and Egypt knew how crazy I was, so I guess that's why she came running out the house looking like she just woke up. She had on some leggings and an oversized tee. I closed my eyes and counted to ten because the shit I was already feeling behind Kilo, and now this was about to send me off the edge.

"Dreon, what is your problem? You can't come here acting like this!" she shouted, stomping her feet and throwing her hands up to her head when I pulled my bat out my trunk.

"*Kill all that noise because you know ME, EGYPT! THIS IS ME, DRIP, and you know how I get when it comes to you. YO, WHAT THE FUCK ARE YOU DOING AT THIS CLOWN'S HOUSE?*" *I yelled as I ran up on her and sandwiched her on the trunk of her car.*

"*Yo, back up off her, homie,*" *Pras said, trying to step up in between us. I dropped the bat and delivered a right hook to his jaw, sending him to the ground cradling his face like a bitch.*

"*IS THIS THE NIGGA YOU'RE CHOOSING?*" *I screamed, letting spit fly out like a maniac. I was way past my limit, and Egypt looked terrified.*

"*Fuck you, nigga. That's why when your bitch needed someone, I was there with a shoulder to cry and dick to ride on!*" *Pras shouted, still holding his jaw and standing to his feet.*

I was ready to charge at him, but Egypt pushed me back hard as hell, causing me to flex at her ass, and she jumped back quick in fear.

"*Oh, so you protecting this nigga? Tell me, Egypt, did you fuck him?*" *I yelled, stepping back into her face.*

"*YOU DON'T LIKE IT, DO IT? I WAS SICK AS A DOG AND ALL I WANTED SHIT ALL I NEEDED WAS YOU, YET YOU DIDN'T COME HOME, AND I COULDN'T GET IN TOUCH WITH YOU. I DROVE TO ALL THE PLACES I FIGURED YOU BE, INCLUDING THE DEALERSHIP DRIP AND THAT BITCH ASS RECEPTIONIST TOLD ME SHE PREGNANT BY YOU, NIGGA. TIME AND TIME AGAIN DRIP, I HAVE FORGIVEN YOU, AND YOU PROMISE THAT YOU A CHANGE. YO ASS A LIE YOU AIN'T NEVER GONE CHANGE. SHIT DOESN'T FEEL GOOD TO HAVE YOUR HEART CRUSHED, HUH?*" *she yelled at the top of her lungs, crushing me with each word.*

"*So that's the type time you on right now, E? Damn, not my Egypt. Yo, I can't even deal with this shit. Our family is laid up in the hospital fighting for his life, and you out here being a hoe on some spiteful get back shit. You flaw as fuck for that bogus ass shit. But, I'm a let you rock though how you want you got it, E." I threw her the deuces and hopped in my ride. She came running to my car banging on the window, yelling for me to wait, but I was good on her and this bullshit, fuck that.*

"That bitch was lying too, but I hope that lie was worth it, and that revenge dick was good to you," I said through the window I had rolled down before pulling off. I could see her yelling up in Pras' face and then hopping in her car and coming down the street behind me, heading in the same direction that I was driving in.

Edge

I was racking my brain trying to find out who would do this shit to Kilo. I had some people out trying to gather information, and I was also trying to keep Tori calm because she was stressing that the shit I'd done to Saga bitch ass was the cause of all this. I was sick of seeing my sister so broken up, hurt, and trying to console her was hard. Mrs. Lolly ended up being a match, and I knew that things were gone turn out good for my boy. I pulled Kilo back into this life so that he could level up and be good. We had our hands in the streets, but we had legit businesses, so we weren't out here just for nothing.

I started to think about all the times I lied to Louve about what I did for income. I had started a storm of bullshit with my lies, trying to protect my sister. I had a father in jail fighting to get a 25-year sentence reduced, and a fucked mother out here living her life on drugs on the street. I had so much pain and anger built up for the way my mom left us and let drugs be more important than her family. She was the precise reason I was scared to commit fully, but Tori was it for me, and now we had a wedding to plan and get ready for.

I wanted kids and a wife to come home to, and at 35, I wasn't getting no younger. I loved the way she loved my family and me with no ill intentions. She held me down and pushed me to do better and be better. We meshed with little problems, and the few we had was usually my fault for dealing with these bum ass girls out here.

Looking around the waiting room, I realized the severity of this shit for real. We were camped out waiting for the outcome of the blood transfusion and surgery that Kilo was having. That could be in there right now, and life was too short to live watching over your shoulder.

Louve kept going to the reception desk and whispering to the nurse, and I was starting to get worried that shit was bad with Kilo, and she was hiding it. I waited as she spoke to another nurse or aide and then came back over to where we all were in the waiting room. She sat down, bouncing her leg and nervously biting her nails. I got up and went over to where she was sitting. I pulled her close and hugged her to let her know I was here, and she wasn't in this alone. I had never seen Louve like this, and not being able to make it better for her like I have done all the times that she needed me to do was killing me.

I was about to ask Louve what the nurses were saying and what they were discussing, but the nurse rushed over before I could speak.

"Ms. Luxe, your mother is awake! I told her how you had been here waiting for her to awake all week, and she broke down crying and asked for me to get you," the nurse stated without stopping to take a breath.

"Wait, hold up. Louve, what is this lady talking about your mom? Is she talking about our mom? I questioned Louve intensely.

"I'm sorry you had to find out like this Edge, but daddy knew you wouldn't want to help mom, so he sent me to find her and help. Well, when I went to where Uncle Vern said she had been staying, I was sent here because she was in a medically induced coma," she replied, wiping away some tears.

I didn't know what to say, but Louve grabbed my hand and led me to the elevator. I was in shock and at a loss for words while also being mad that no one told me. My pops had just talked to me this morning and never mentioned shit. I saw Uncle Vern yesterday, and Louve could have easily told me and let me in in this.

During the elevator ride, I felt like the same little boy I was when our mother left us for good. We got off the elevator and reached the room, but we stood outside, and Louve blocked the entrance.

"Edge, she is still our beautiful mother, but she has lost a lot of weight hair, and she looks like a zombie," she warned.

"It's cool, Louve. I won't be rude or judge her I'm a act cool and like I have some sense left hahaha. But, for real, this shit that we are going through with Kilo has me looking at a lot of things differently. Life too short, Lou Lou," I stated, kissing her forehead.

We walked in the room, but it was empty, and all our mothers' things were gone. I locked eyes with Louve, and we knew she had left and was back out in the streets, and I felt like that kid again getting excited to see a mother you love but never is around. Louve broke down in tears, and all I could do was hold my sister. Today was a rough ass day, and the night was not even over yet.

Chapter One

LOUVE

I couldn't control the tears that were rapidly falling from my eyes, and I felt myself about to have a panic attack. Edge squeezed my hand tight, pulling me in for a hug. I was devastated as I looked at the empty room that once held my hope for mending my relationship with my mother. We turned to leave the room and walked right into the night nurse I had grown close to. She was bringing in more supplies to stock the room back up.

"Ms. Luxe, what's wrong sweetie?" she asked, handing me some tissues.

"I'm just disappointed that my mother left, and after everything she has done, I thought we'd finally fix our family," I cried, unable to stop my emotions from taking over.

"Wait, sweetie, you have it all wrong. We moved Loucille to the second-floor rehab wing. Once she woke up and all the tests came back ok, we moved her to start physical therapy right away," she replied, smiling wide.

I was so shocked but happy as she gave us the correct room number. I looked at Edge, and he held a nervous expression as we headed out of the room and back to the elevator. Time went in slow motion as we waited for the elevator to arrive. The elevator chimed, and we stepped on. The door closed, and we rode in silence. I could hear my heart racing fast, beating out my chest. The elevator chimed, and the doors opened. We both looked at each other and then stepped off, me first, and Edge followed. This floor smelled better than the others did, and the colors were bright and fun, not dark and gloomy like the pale blue on the other floors.

We walked slowly observing the patients engaged in various therapy activities. There was music playing lowly, a bit upbeat, and fun. My palms were sweating, and my head felt like I was spinning around. I was beyond nervous, and I needed to get something to drink to quench my parched mouth. I stopped at a vending machine and grabbed a bottle of water. I drank damn near the whole bottle in one gulp. I wiped my mouth with the back of my hand and placed the cap back on the bottle. It was now or never. The room was two doors away from where we both stood lost in our thoughts.

"You ready?" I nervously asked Edge.

He never responded. He just grabbed my hand, and we walked inside the room.

Chapter Two

DRIP

I drove in complete silence once I lost Egypt a few turns back. I was too pissed to head up to the hospital just yet, so I sent Edge a text letting him know I was heading home for a few and to hit me if any word or update on Kilo. Damn, man, my nigga, Killa Kilo got to pull through this shit. Today's events got my ass stressed to the fucking max. To be honest and keep it a buck, a nigga is down bad over this shit with Egypt.

I changed for her, and one lie from some bird sent her off to the next nigga. Visions of that clown ass nigga touching her invaded my mind repeatedly, and I needed to get to my stash of Kush and my Henny — the only way I was gone be able to cope right now because I wanted to go back and murk that nigga just off the fact he was sniffing around my girl. It may not have been the correct way to handle this shit and cope with shit at the moment, but with everything happening at once, it was the way I was choosing to take these L's that life was sending my way.

I hadn't seen or talked to my G-Mama in a minute, and I knew the minute I stepped foot in her house, she was gone light into my ass with the quickness. I had been hitting Muse up way before this shit with Kilo popped off, and he was M.I.A. Although Muse was my cousin, we weren't as close as we used to be, and although he said he had no issues behind Kilo and me leaving the Hittas, I was starting to feel like that was bullshit. Before we stopped running with him and his crew, he was around always, and we always were turning up or just chilling at the strip club. Now, it's been months since I even got a call from him let alone seen him.

I was gone check on my G-Mama and see if Muse had been by to check up on her. If G-Mama ain't from Muse, then I was gone have to slide through his building and make sure he was straight. Shit, either way, I was gone have to pull up on him to see what his issue was. My first visit would be G-Mama because I needed advice from her in the worst way. She was my heart and the woman who raised me. She was my voice of reason, especially when the beast in me needed to be tamed.

I could literally call up a few bad bitches like I used to do, and revenge fuck my stress away, but I wasn't interested in them. My soul was bruised, and my heart was crushed. Man, we'll do our women foul as hell and take them through the most shit, but I am living proof that if they do the same even one time, it hurts deeply to the core. I arrived at my hideaway and headed inside. I kicked off my Yeezy's at the door and went right to the bar for my fifth of Henny and my pre-rolled blunts.

I sat on the stool at my bar and began my routine. I poured up a shot of Henny, tossed it back, sparked up my blunt, and let the gas immediately take over my stress. I opened my eyes after my first pull of the blunt and stared at the picture of Egypt I had in her bikini on the beach in Mexico from the trip we took. She glowed in the sun in the yellow bikini with her wild curls wet and falling to her shoulders. She had no clue that I was snapping mad pictures of her from the balcony of our villa. I had wrapped up a call and an early meeting to come to kick it with her and found her on the beach enjoying the sun and water. I seized the opportunity to capture her in her natural beauty, and the essence of her had my mind blown. I framed the best picture out of about 50 that I took and placed it right here where I could keep her close.

This girl was my world and had my damn heart. I had the urge to throw the frame up against the wall, but I just grabbed the Henny bottle and took it straight to the head no chaser. I had sat here in the same spot, never moving just drinking this liquor like a bottle of water. The more I thought of Egypt, and what she did, I drank. I basically took a sip every minute because she was embedded in my mind and never leaving. I was starting to feel that tingly feeling and I knew I was close to being lifted off the Kush and liquor. I was hoping the feelings would numb, but it seemed to do the opposite because feelings were intensified, and I felt like I had lost Egypt and it was no coming back.

I played games with Egypt so many times that maybe this was Karma for my ass. I had finally stuck to the straight and narrow and was ready to be 100% committed, and my ass got played in the worse way. I wanted to go get her and figure this shit out, but the thought alone of that nigga Pras having her weighed heavy on the decision to let her ass go completely. I don't know if I'm built to deal with her and look past her fucking another nigga. I was hoping she'd plead her case and tell me I had it all wrong, but she was talking tough like she got some get-back on my ass with revenge dick.

I ain't been a saint in the least bit, but Egypt was an angel in my eyes, and to know I did so much dirt that pushed her to change who she was just to get me back was a hard pill to swallow. My gut was telling me that she didn't fuck that clown, and that was trying to get under my skin, which she for damn sure had done. And with those thoughts and gut instincts, my pride and bruised ego wouldn't allow me to reach out to her and clear the air. I was a stubborn ass Taurus bull at heart, and that shit was true as hell today. I just couldn't bring myself to face her. So instead, I'd drown my pain and anger with these drinks and blunts.

Chapter Three

EGYPT

Drip was going to make me hurt his petty ass when it's all said and done. This nigga drops a bomb about someone being in the hospital fighting for their life but never told me who or what the hell happened. His rude ass just hops in the car and takes off forcing me to have to try to follow him to the hospital only for him to purposely lose me a few turns back. I was beyond frustrated and worried as hell wondering what happened and who it happened to.

I decided to pull over instead just driving aimlessly with no destination. I pulled into the first shell gas station I saw. I pulled my cell phone out my purse and powered it back on. I could kick my own ass for powering my cell off and never thinking to turn it back on. I wanted to avoid talking to Drip and now look what the hell happens. I was regretting everything I had done yesterday to make him hurt like I was hurting, but I'm still hurting and now even more. Seeing the hurt look on his face broke my heart.

As soon as my Note 9 fully powered on, multiple notifications started to chime in back to back from FB, IG, email, and texts. The first message I opened was a group message from Louve. The thread was damn near 50 messages, but the first one told me all I needed to know. I immediately felt like shit. I tossed the phone in the passenger seat and started my car up to head over to the hospital. I started to pray the minute I was back in traffic dipping in and out of lanes. I prayed for Kilo to be protected and pull through this. I was a ball of nerves driving and fighting back the tears along with trying to fight the nausea I was still feeling. I arrived at the hospital, pulling right up to ER entrance, quickly parking the car, and then running inside.

I ran straight to the ER reception desk and was directed to the waiting room. I searched the room looking for the family. I turned the corner of an area by the vending machines, and my eyes fell on the family all seated in various places throughout the room. The majority of the crew was camped out sleep in weird positions in the chairs or on the benches, and the kids were scattered about the floor and chairs. Edge and Louve were nowhere in sight and, I didn't see Drip. I made a mental note to try to check on him. I was concerned because Drip wasn't good with dealing with his emotions, and I know he was hurting right now behind Kilo being shot. Knowing Drip though, he was gone hold a grudge and be petty for a while.

I took the empty seat next to Tori. She was sleeping in the chair in the corner of the waiting room with her head rested against a small pillow propped up on the wall. I nudged her softly, and she didn't budge, so I nudged her a bit harder than I actually meant to, and she shot up straight in her chair eyes wide and bulging looking at me like she was scared as hell. She rubbed her eyes while I snickered at how crazy she looked. She finally settled down and looked at me. Her eyes were bloodshot red, and her usually neat top knot was in and unkempt messy bun. She had on a hoodie with leggings and fur slides.

"Hey boo, what's the word on Kilo?" I asked while looking around the waiting area. I had the worst feeling, and I hated hospitals.

"Hey boo, it's about time your ass got here. Anyway, after we all tried to donate blood and weren't a match, Ms. Lolly volunteered to donate and felt she would be a match since she is Kilo's paternal grandmother. Yea, I see the wheels turning in your head. That's a whole story for another time. Nevertheless, she was indeed a match, thankfully. Kilo was still in surgery last, I knew. We just waiting for an update," she replied, stretching and yawning.

I didn't respond because honestly, I was speechless, and it was all a lot to take in. I sat all the way back in the seat and laid my head on the wall. Today had been stressful as hell and not a good start to my morning. I silenced my ringing phone and rejected Pras' call. I quickly blocked his number before he could call back. That was a chapter I needed to close because it was nothing going to come from it. I accepted his invite out of spite, and it was proving to be a bad idea. He now thought I was interested in him and the shit he started up with Dreon didn't do shit but piss me off, so his ass was grass from here on out.

I couldn't get this nausea to subside, and the shit was irking me for the last few days. I don't know what I was coming down with, but I wanted it to be done already. The nausea was starting to intensify by the seconds, and I was beginning to feel hot. The room was spinning as I began to feel dizzy. I needed to get some water and to a bathroom before I threw up in the waiting room. As soon as I stood up, I felt myself losing my balance. I tried to take a step but didn't make it far as I started to fall. I felt myself hit the floor, but I was unable to see my vision had become blurry, and I was feeling like I was having an out-of-body experience as I heard everyone screaming around me.

Chapter Four

TORI

I frantically dialed Edge after trying to reach Drip a countless number of times and to no avail. Egypt had passed out, and they rushed her back to a room in the ER to check on her and figure out what was wrong with her. Today was just too damn much, and I was on the verge of losing my damn mind. The phone rang over to voicemail, and I was irritated as hell because I couldn't reach anyone. I shot a quick text to Edge and Louve about Egypt, and then I sent a text to Ms. Lolly letting her know I'd be in the ER waiting area where they took Egypt. Kilo was in the still trauma unit, and we were still waiting on his update. I sent up continuous prayers for him to pull through this.

As soon as I sat down and started scrolling on my phone to pass the time and calm my nerves, a nurse came out looking for me. I walked the hall following close behind her as she led the way to the ER room that Egypt was in. The hall was dark, cold, and smelled like death and germs. Whatever that smelled like, I equated it to this smell right here. We reached the room, and she let me go in as she turned around and left. I stepped around the curtain, and Egypt was sitting up in the bed with her head down and chin resting into her chest with tears falling down her face and onto her hospital gown. She was holding some papers and a folder in her hand that she was staring at as she cried.

"Egypt, boo, what's wrong?" I asked while taking a seat on the bed next to her and pulling her in for a hug.

She didn't speak a word, but once she placed the contents from her hands into mine, no words were needed as I looked at the sonogram in my hand of her growing baby.

"I wasn't expecting this news at all Tori, but it makes sense with all the symptoms I have. However, this is supposed to be a happy moment for me, and I am a mess. Drip is pissed with me, and the hurt I caused showed all in his eyes when I was at Pras' house where he found me," she blurted out while still balling in tears.

I rubbed her back as she told me what happened this morning between her and Drip. I had to hold my laugh in when she said Drip knocked Pras' bitch ass down and when Drip purposely lost her in traffic on the way here. Drip was so damn petty it ain't make no sense.

"It will be good, sis. Just let King Petty cool his ass off. But, I do have a question, boo. Did you sleep with Pras? I asked her while holding my breath waiting on an answer.

"No, I didn't, but he tried and probably would have if I had any more drinks in me. I passed out on his couch and woke up after only two hours of sleep to Drip banging on the door, but that's the least of my worries. Sis, I have to tell you something, and you have to promise to not say anything to anyone at all, especially pillow talking with Edge," Egypt said, giving me a serious expression.

"Yes, boo, of course, I promise," I replied and listened closely as she began to tell me the story. The more she told me, my eyes grew wide as saucers, and my mouth dropped open as I clutched my invisible pearls.

This was some deep shit, and I had no clue how we were going to get her out of this, but I promised to help her out. The wheels started to turn, and I began to think that Kilo's shooting might be connected to this and Saga's death. Shit was about to get real around here, and although I promised not to tell, I think we were going to have to call for some help on this shit. I still had my girl's back, but we needed reinforcement in this situation, and it was going to have to be outside the crew. I wouldn't tell Edge and Drip, but I had to call someone, and I knew just who to call. We had to boss the fuck up and handle this before another one of us or someone close to us ends up dead, or in the same situation as Kilo.

Chapter Five

EDGE

I sat off to the side as Louve and our mother Loucille hugged tightly. She looked full of life having Louve in her arms, but she was skinny. My mother was never a thin woman. She had meat on her bones and was a nice healthy size woman back in the day, so it's hard as hell to see her like this now so frail and fragile. I was battling a thousand and one emotions. I wanted to engage in the hugs and be joyful to have found our mother after all this time, but I couldn't ignore the hurt that I was feeling. I wanted to know why she chose drugs over her own kids. How could she leave her family like that for all those years?

I wasn't ready to hug her, but I was prepared to get some answers from her. Once her and Louve let go of their embrace and grabbed tissues to wipe their tears, I took that as my opportunity to get down to the issues at hand. It might have been the wrong time to be addressing these concerns, but I waited years for the chance, and who knew if she'd stick around. The least she could do was give us an explanation. I needed to know her intentions as well now that we were reunited. Before I could fully let my guard down with

Loucille, I had to get this out the way. I cleared my throat getting their attention. They looked over at me, so I let it out.

"You might not be ready to answer these questions, but I need answers to the things you did and the pain you caused. You know like make it make sense for me, Loucille. Why did you choose drugs over us? How could you leave us for years and never even care to come check on us? What type of mother leaves her own kids her own flesh and blood?" I yelled while trying to hold back the tears that I hadn't let out since the day she left. I had held them in staying strong.

She fumbled her hands around in her lap and closed her eyes tightly taking in deep breaths before speaking.

"Have you ever lost control of yourself and of your life or who you were? I thought that I was no good for you guys and that maybe while I was so lost and in bad shape that the one thing I could do was spare you guys the haunting memories of a drug-addicted mother. I felt like my presence would have done more harm, so I stayed away. I thought I was protecting you, Edge. I was no good for myself, so how could I be good for you two. I thought I could battle this shit and get better on my own and come back, but before I knew it, weeks became months, and that turned to years. I only got worse, and I never expected this habit to spiral so far out of control. This fall and hospital stay have been a blessing in disguise and literally knocked some sense into me.

I will be going into a rehab center in two weeks once I'm fully healed and cleared by my neurologist. I will do this for me most importantly so I can be better for my family. With the help of you and Louve, I know I can overcome this. I have grandchildren who I want and need to be a grandmother to. I want my husband and kids back in my life where we all belong," she replied, still crying heavily in between.

I heard all I needed to hear, and I would take it with a

grain of salt due to her track record with us. I left her and Louve to talk while I went to check on the family and Kilo. The time had gone by fast as hell, and I couldn't believe how long we had been gone from everyone. I powered my phone on, and it started to go crazy with text messages and voice-mails. I started reading the texts from Tori, and I rushed back in to tell Louve we had to get back downstairs and see what the hell was going on. She kissed our mother and promised her we would be back before we rushed off to the elevator.

Chapter Six

LOUVE

Two Weeks Later

I was a nervous wreck as I watched Kilo lay in the hospital bed. He slipped into a coma after surgery and had yet to wake up. The surgeon was able to remove all the bullets safely, including the one that was left from the first shooting. Although the surgery and blood transfusion was successful, and he was expected to make a full recovery, his body was tired and basically defended itself by going into a coma to heal. It was now on Kilo to wake up from this when his body was ready. I hated to see him like this, and especially with how things were with us prior to the shooting and crash. I hadn't seen him in a while and seeing him this way made me angry with myself for running off how I did.

The doctors told us that Kilo was lucky to have survived through the shooting and car accident. I prayed for him more than I ever have, and I knew the moment he woke up, we'd get our chance to make things right. I stayed here around the clock day in and day out just praying and waiting for Kilo to wake up. The family came by daily sometimes twice a day to check on Kilo and me. The kids were missing us at home and couldn't wait to be a family again. If it wasn't for Ms. Lolly, I don't know what we would do. She was a godsend to our family, and I was grateful to have her. School was about to let out soon for the summer in about two weeks, and I needed to find some camps and different programs to keep the kids active and busy.

I had my doctor's appointment today, and although I was ten weeks now, the baby measured way smaller than that, and to top it off, my blood pressure was up high as hell. I prayed that I didn't suffer another miscarriage behind all this stress I was dealing with like the last time. I barely slept or even ate how I should, but I had no appetite and could not sleep well while Kilo was in a coma. Between crying and praying, I was mentally exhausted and drained. I took on bathing and massaging Kilo just as the nurses had taught me to do over the last few days. From the beginning, I had taken so many notes and paid close attention, always asking questions until I was able to take over.

I Face Timed Ms. Lolly and the kids and talked to them for a few. This was the norm now, and our routine was going ok, but I was ready for Kilo to come back to me. I emailed the social worker at the rehab center to check on my mama. Edge had paid for everything at the best rehab facility in California. Although I talked to her on the phone, I still needed to verify with the staff that she was following the rules and doing well. I had faith in her, but I couldn't lie and say I wasn't nervous that she would up and disappear on us again one day. I prayed she would get the care and healing that she needed to get clean and stay that way.

Edge, on the other hand, was a lost cause at this point. I had decided just to let go of trying to get him to talk to mama and focus on me and her building our relationship. Unfortunately, Edge was stubborn as hell and true to his Taurus sign. Edge could hold a grudge forever, especially if you hurt him, so a part of me wasn't even surprised at how he was handling our mama.

Edge said he was treading lightly with her and waiting it out to see if she would stick it out in rehab before he put his all back into her. My father was beyond happy that we had located mama and got her to go to rehab. He thanked me every time we talked for putting our family back together. Things were looking good with my father's case, and I kept prayers going up for him as well.

My father had an appeal hearing coming up soon, and since the judge and prosecutors from his case were under fire for setting up African American suspects but letting off the white suspects with the same or very similar charges, it was looking promising for him. I pray that they free him, and then our family really can be complete and back together again. All of this was fueling my drive to push forward and not break and give up. Every day was a struggle and mental battle to keep my faith and positive vibe.

I tossed my phone on the ottoman in between my feet that I had them propped up on top of. I was growing sick and tired of calling Drip only to get his voicemail, which was now full of the countless voicemails I had left him over the last few days. I was contemplating on pulling up on him at his hideout loft that he thought I knew nothing about. I knew I couldn't go there and really show my ass because for one I'm pregnant, and for two, the loft is in a nice ass area, and they will surely call the cops my yellow ass. I had been pissed off for days, and even more so now at the shit that I found out.

I had come home the other night after the test results of my blood work showed no type of birth control in my system and went right to my birth control pills to inspect them. My doctor basically told me I hadn't been taking any birth control, so the pregnancy was fine and healthy with no concerns. My gut told me this had Drip's name all over it. He was so damn petty, and I knew that he could do some crazy shit like switching out my pills. That put my mind into overdrive to find out what the hell I had been consuming then because I most definitely and faithfully took my birth control pills around the clock.

I rushed home to inspect the pack of birth control pills. I was livid when I realize that the times where I was sending Drip to pick up my prescription from the pharmacy, and his ass was swapping my medicine with allergy pills instead.

This nigga had set my ass up and trapped me with a baby but was missing in action now on my ass. I never revealed on any of the voicemails that I left him that I was, in fact, pregnant because I felt that was a face-to-face conversation to have as adults. Even with the anger that I was feeling, I was truly missing him like crazy. The house was empty and quiet as hell without him and Homie. I was in a miserable, lonely state in life right now, and I was tired of this. This pregnancy is supposed to be happy and stress-free.

Even the crew wasn't the same. Everyone was distant and trying to deal with the curve balls life had thrown us. We all were praying and waiting for Kilo to wake up out the coma any day. This situation was horrible, and it was an eye-opener for me, and I hope everyone else, including Drip. Life was too short to waste being mad, petty, and fighting when we could be gone at any time, wishing we could go back in time and do it over. I was going to put my pride aside and fight for my man because I loved him deeply to the bottom of my heart.

I needed to go and talk to him, and he was going to listen to today, enough was enough. He got me pregnant like he wanted and now was the perfect time to fix this shit storm of a relationship. We had a little over seven months before we welcomed a baby into the world, and we needed to be a unit and raise our baby in a loving environment with no more petty ass games.

I was looking forward to a fun and poppin' ass summer,

and now it was about to be a long hot ass summer pregnant and on lock in Cali. He knew exactly what he was trying to do when he did this shit at this time. He hated it when I went out with my friends and turned up. He preferred me home and waiting on his ass, and that's exactly what I'd do if I'm knocked up, so he decided to play dirty as hell. I was pissed, but I had to laugh at this crazy ass shit he done pulled.

I hopped up and hurried upstairs to change my clothes. I was in a hurry, but I wasn't about to head out the house in no pajamas. I opted for my biker shorts, a racer back tank over my sports bra, and my Nike slides. I snatched my fanny pack and keys and was on my way. I pulled the door open looking down at my phone only to walk into a figure. I looked up and was stopped in my tracks by an unwelcomed guest.

I saw the look in his eyes, and he seemed off, and a bit crazed looking. I have known this man a long time and never saw this look, but I wasn't trying to figure it out today wasn't the day.

"I don't have time to talk today, so I'll reach out to you later," I said as I locked the door.

I went to step around him and was grabbed quickly, and a cloth was placed over my mouth and nose. The scent was strong, so I held my breath to keep from inhaling the chemicals. I was lifted into the air, and he began to try to carry me down the stairs, but I kicked and fought while still holding my breath. It was a struggle to not breathe in the fumes on the cloth as he tightened his grip over my face. I swung my foot as far back as I could under me kicking him in the nuts. He dropped me instantly and rolled down the stairs as he yelled out in agony and pain, holding his groin.

I didn't even feel the impact of me hitting the pavement and landing on my back. I hopped up and ran full speed to my car in the driveway. I immediately locked the car and glanced at the front of the house as I started the car, and he was gone. It was as if he had vanished into thin air. I didn't have time to figure that out. I had to get out here. I dialed Tori, and she didn't answer. I frantically drove and fumbled around with my phone. I felt myself growing weak and feeling faint as I drove like a madwoman to Drip's place. I turned on my AC to try to keep myself up. I drove as fast as I could and trying my hardest not to pass out or crash. I reached Drip's condo and saw his car parked in the lot, so I pulled in next to him and quickly parked.

I got out on wobbly legs and finally made my way up the stairs and to his building. I pushed the bell frantically while looking around to see if I was followed at all. My mouth was growing dry, and my body was feeling weaker by the minute.

"What the fuck are you doing here, E? I can see yo ass on the video monitor!" Drip yelled, sounding frustrated.

"Please help me, Dreon," I cried out weakly.

No response was given, and I had no more energy to hold myself up, so I collapsed dropping down to the brick ground and resting my body up against the door for support. I felt myself slowing fading and about to pass out. Tears flooded my eyes as I realized I was alone and on my own with no help.

The door swung open, almost knocking me over. I looked up and locked eyes with Drip, and I saw the hurt and pain in his eyes and all on his face, but as he looked me over, I saw the care and love come to the forefront. I felt that love as he scooped me up and carried me inside.

"What the hell is going on, Egypt? Are you drunk?" he asked me as we entered his condo and sat me on the couch.

I was stuck because I wanted to tell him everything, including the secrets of my past. I was frozen with silence as I stared up at him standing over me talking. Everything he was saying was now sounding like I was underwater and my eyes involuntarily began to roll up into my eyelids. The room felt as if someone spun a wheel, and I was attached to it. I couldn't see clearly or make out the words he was speaking, but I could feel him shaking me hard before everything went black.

Chapter Eight

DRIP

I paced back and forth as Nurse Audrey, our personal hood nurse, checked out Egypt. I was lost as hell as to what was wrong and why the hell she passed out. Thinking quickly, I called up Audrey since she stays in the same subdivision instead of taking a trip to the hospital. I had got her to wake up, but she was out of it and groggy. She kept going in and out of consciousness, and that was freaking me out. I didn't know if she had alcohol poisoning or took some damn pills. I never took Egypt to be that type of female, but nowadays, you just never know.

Audrey came in and hooked up all this portable equipment that was driving me crazy because every noise had me worried that it meant something was wrong. She kicked me out of the room and sent me to the living room where I was currently on edge as I waited for an update. Audrey finally peeked her head out waving m back in. Egypt was awake and finally stable and talking. I came to the door and looked her over. She looked a little pale, but her beauty was captivating to me. She had this pure essence and aura about her that I missed.

I needed some answers, and I was impatient as hell, but I decided to wait for Audrey to exit before I opened that can of worms. Audrey packed her things up and handed Egypt a script for iron pills. They hugged and said their goodbyes, and I walked Audrey to the door. I pulled out a few blue faces and passed them to Audrey.

"Thank you, Audrey. I appreciate you, ma," I said, hugging her and opening the door.

"You're welcome, Dreon. I appreciate the side money. It helps with these student loans that are killing my pockets. Keep her hydrated, and if she faints again, call me but get her to the ER," she replied, pulling her bag out by the handle as it rolled behind her on the wheels. I locked up and went back to talk to Egypt.

I walked into the room, and it was completely silent now that all the equipment was gone. The tension in the room was thick as hell between us, and neither of us had spoken a word yet. I needed the answers to questions that were burning to come out, so I said fuck it and spoke first.

"Did you try to kill yourself, E?" I asked, sitting on the end of the bed with my back to her.

I looked straight ahead out the window at the night sky. I couldn't look her in her face just yet after all that had tran-spired over the last few weeks. I was on pins and needles as I waited for her to respond to my question. I prayed the shit was a mishap and not her trying to off herself. If she said she was trying to do that, I'd be checking her into a facility ASAP for mental help.

"No, Dreon, I didn't try to kill myself. I would never do anything like that, and you know that. Yea, I'm hurt behind our shit, but I ain't that damn hurt to harm myself," she replied with an attitude.

"So, what happened today, E? Because Audrey thinks it's more to it than what you are saying, and so do I. It seemed like your ass was high out your mind on some shit," I stated loudly still seated with my back to her.

"I was attacked, and this man tried to make me pass out from some chemicals on a cloth. I fought and held my breath, and I must have accidentally inhaled the fumes as I was fighting to get him off me. I kicked him in the balls and took off the minute he let me go. I hopped in my car and came straight here, and it's like he disappeared out of thin air because as I sped out my driveway he was gone nowhere to be found," she sobbed as she told me.

I felt myself growing hot as I took in everything she said. The ringing of her phone interrupted my thoughts. Her fanny pack laid on my dresser where her phone was. I got up, and I grabbed it and then handed it to her. She rummaged around through it spilling out the contents until she retrieved her phone from the bottom of the bag. I bent down to pick up the items that fell from the bed to the floor. I handed her the Chap Stick pen and some small papers. I pulled the papers back when I focused my eyes on what was in my hand. I noticed that it was some type of image. Upon pulling it closer to my face for inspection, I realized that it was a sonogram with her information from the hospital dated a few weeks ago.

I looked at the image for so long not paying her any attention as I let it settle in that this was a baby in her stomach that I was looking at. It wasn't much to make out because it was small, but it was, in fact, a baby there. I finally looked at her, and our eyes met, and she looked scared as hell as I stared at her. I wanted to be excited and let it show that I was happy as hell, but then that sick feeling hit me like a ton of bricks. What if this wasn't my baby?

"Surprise, we're pregnant. I've been calling you since the day we had the blow-up, that's when I found out, and I wanted to share it with in person." She played with her hands as she nervously looked at me, waiting for me to respond.

"Whose baby is it? Mine or that punk ass nigga whose house you was at?" I calmly said while keeping a straight face.

"ARE YOU SERIOUS, DREON? Hahaha, this is your damn baby, and you know damn well it is seeing as how you trapped me. You switched my fucking birth control pills with allergy over-the-counter meds and have the nerves to question me about whose baby it is when you a whole trap star out here. Yes, I was at Pras' house, but I never slept with him, and I was there all of three hours when you showed up because I was too damn tipsy to drive. Had your dumb ass been answering and not going missing in action, I would have never even ended up anywhere looking for your ass!" she screamed, jumping up from the bed and grabbing the lamp on the nightstand and launching it at my head.

I moved just in time before it connected with my head, but it hit the wall and shattered into pieces.

"Aye, calm your hyper ass down, and don't be throwing shit at me in my house, breaking shit you ain't buy. I asked the damn question because your extra friendly ass was up in a nigga's house and nowhere to be found. Then when I did find your ass there, you were popping big shit to me insinuating that you were doing the shit that I'd done to you, so you damn right I asked if it's my damn seed. My bad if I offended you E, but you not innocent," I stated, sitting on the bed again with my back to her.

"Yea, well, like I said I never slept with him. I only let him help me out with my car out of spite and because I thought that Kelli chick was telling the truth. Plus, you weren't answering your phone, so I took all that and ran with shit. I ain't happy about it, but I learned my lesson, and I apologize," she replied just above a whisper, but I heard her loud and clear.

"Do you know who the motherfucka is that attacked you?" I asked, finally turning around to look at her.

"No, he wore a ski mask, and when I got to my car, he was gone," she replied, looking at her hands.

"Well, you gone to stay here with me until we find a new house. It's some weird shit going on with Kilo getting shot then ran off the road, and now this. I'm not taking any chances. You might as well tell work you're out for a while. I need to keep you close at all times, and you need rest for my baby and stop passing out. I'm a send someone to check on the house and grab you some shit and bring it here. We can rent it out or put it up for sale. Just let me know, and I'll contact a realtor," I said, getting up to go order us some food and make some calls.

"Dreon, say something about the baby and us?" she yelled out, stopping me in my tracks at the door.

I turned around, and she was climbing out of bed. She came over to me and grabbed my face looking me deep in my eyes, waiting on me to answer her. We just stared at each other, not speaking any words. Fuck it! I love this girl and have been sick without her.

I pulled her into me and kissed her deeply, letting our tongues get reacquainted. She untied my basketball shorts and tugged at them with my boxers to get them down. My dick was hard as hell and stopping her from getting them off. I pulled them down and stepped out of them, and she was already out of her clothes. She looked sexy as hell, and I couldn't wait any longer to feel her.

I picked her up and slid her dripping wet center down on my pole. She was hot and tight, and I had to pause and bite my lip to keep myself from cumming in minutes. I'd miss the smell and feel of her and wanted to savor this feeling.

Egypt had other plans and started grinding on my pole as I held onto her hips. I had to back up into the dresser to hold myself up. She was giving my ass some work bucking on me like she was riding a bull. I had to steady her before she had me in here screaming like a bitch. I watched her as she threw her head back, placing both feet on the dresser to steady herself. I couldn't take much more of letting her fuck me, so I took control and carried her to the bed. I laid her on the bed, and I pulled her to the edge of my bed and bent her legs back as I dived into taste the honey that flowed from her pot. I let her legs free as I squeezed her breasts, but she told me they were sore. She kept tightening her legs around my neck, so I snatched her up and flipped her upside in my arms letting her legs rest on my shoulder as I locked them in place with my arms wrapped around each one.

I feasted on her like I was starving and let all her juices flow in my mouth. I don't know what had gotten into us, but we were going at it like porn stars in this motherfucka. I started to tease her clit with my tongue as I traced circles around it with the tip of my tongue.

"Oohhhh fuck, Drip! That feels so good baby, I missed you!" she moaned out in pure satisfaction.

I almost lost my damn balance when she started to kiss the head of my dick with her soft lips. She slowly slid it into her mouth while suctioning tight like a vacuum. The more I sucked and slurped on her center, the more she went wild on my shit with her mouth. We were in a battle to please each other. She started to massage my balls as she let the tip of my dick hit the back of her throat, and I knew it was a wrap. I had to take control back. I flipped her back around, and we kissed hungrily. I climbed into the bed with her still in my arms, and we went at it like we'd been apart for longer than a few weeks.

The shit we were beefing about was irrelevant now. I had my woman back, and all in my world was good for the time being. We spent hours fucking all over my room to the shower and the living room. We finally ended wrapped in each other's arms on the floor in the living room in front of the fireplace. I looked at her as she slept peacefully, and my body was relaxed just by her presence. I wasn't tense, stressed, or irritable now that we were back good. I rubbed on her small belly and felt so much pride knowing that my baby was growing in there. I had to marry this girl. It was only right she and my child had my last name. I got up and started making calls to my jeweler and travel agent. We were heading to Vegas to get married tomorrow.

———

We drove out the drive-thru as a married couple. Egypt was tired and didn't want to park and go in, so we did it all in the car at the drive-thru window. I had booked us the chairman suite at the Bellagio with no return date because we were staying for as long as Egypt wanted to. We pulled up and let the valet park the Maybach we had rented for the time here. I wanted to make our wedding day and honeymoon night unforgettable. We rode the elevator up to the top floor while we kissed like long lost lovers. Shit, to me, I felt lost when we were apart.

I turned my phone on silent and took Egypt's as well as soon as she started snap chatting and filming the room. I wanted a private and uninterrupted honeymoon night. I had them bring up champagne for me and sparkling grape juice for my pregnant wife. Damn, I was a married man now. I had a wife and a baby on the way, and just yesterday I was on the verge of tears behind thinking she was fucking with the next nigga. I guess you really can't say never because I was for sure we were finished for good. Now I have her for life, and that felt like I won the lottery.

Chapter Nine

LOUVE

It has been four weeks now with Kilo still being in a coma, and I was losing my mind. The only thing good beside my kids was the fact that my mother was making strides in rehab. I had got to talk to her this morning, and she sounded ten times better than she did when she went in. She asked about Edge, and I felt bad because he still had his guard up with her. I gave her Uncle Vern's number and pops mailing address to the jail so that she could write to him. She had spoken with Aunt Zoe, and they planned to take a sister trip as soon as my mom was done with her rehab.

I had missed my opportunity to attend the art course, and I was ok with that because Kilo needed me more. The detectives working his case came by yesterday to the hospital and stated they are still investigating. They gave me his cell phone they retrieved from the scene of the accident, and the screen was broken and blank. The phone range but you couldn't see who was calling. Every time I would answer it, they would hang up. I decided to power it off and let all his calls go to voicemail.

I was stretching his legs and massaging him to keep the circulation and blood flow going. I started to rub his arms, and his hand twitched scaring me. I rubbed his hand, and then he gripped it tightly before stopping abruptly. I rang the nurse's bell, and they came flying in. I told them what had happened, and they said that it was normal, and he can hear us and feel us. He will wake up when is he ready. I wish there were a way to bring him out of this coma.

I finished up rubbing him down in Shea butter and massaging his body when there was a knock at the door.

I looked over and saw a pretty woman standing there in the doorway. I watched how she look from me to Kilo, and her mouth dropped in shock. She never spoke a word but handed me an envelope and turned to leave. I raced out and caught up to her.

"Excuse me, but who are you? How do you know Kilo?" I asked, stopping her path and standing in front of her.

"It's all in the letter. I'm sorry, and I'll be praying for Kilo. Our kids need him," she stated, stepping onto the elevator quickly as a worker with a cart came by blocking me from her.

"What the hell did you just say?" I was yelling, trying to get to the elevator. As the worker passed finally, I raced to the elevator just as the doors closed. I banged my finger on the button to open it back up, but I was too late. The elevator went down.

I was fuming mad, so I raced back to the room and ripped the letter open. I held my breath as I read the letter. With each word, my anger intensified like a pot of boiling water about to overflow. This bitch Naomi had revealed everything in this letter and even included her sonogram and copies of the text messages between her and Kilo. I was sick to my stomach when she said that she was keeping their love child.

She stated she would return to LA after she gave birth to ensure a safe pregnancy away from anyone that might try to harm her or end her pregnancy.

An animalistic scream had escaped my throat and ripped through the room. I had reached my point of no return, and I lost all sense. I started to slap and smack Kilo across his face screaming at him.

"How could you do this to me?" I yelled as the tears fell from my face like a running faucet.

I started to toss shit around the room knocking everything over that I could get my hands on. I saw that his monitor was going crazy, and his vitals were flipping out. I knew my outburst was causing it, but I didn't give a fuck. I snatched the cords out the monitor just as Ms. Lolly came in the room followed by nurses and Tori.

Tori ran over to me upon seeing me and how distraught I appeared. She walked me out of the room before security could come, and she practically dragged me to the elevator. Once inside, I collapsed and let the hurt take over, and the pain rocked me deeply. I knew shit was bad, but I never expected him to get the bitch pregnant. All that hounding me to come home and the whole time his dirty dick ass was still fucking that bitch and raw. I felt so disrespected and played. I was done with Kilo, and I meant that shit with every fiber of my being. He better be praying that they connect his shit and bring his ass back. He can call Naomi to nurse him back to health.

I ran everything down to Tori and saying it aloud and seeing her expression only made the shit more real and hurt more. She hugged me tightly as I began to cry and hyperventilate at the sad ass story I had told. I was a mess, and my life was in shambles yet again behind Kilo and his shit. Fool me once shame on you, but fool me twice shame on my silly ass.

We got to the parking lot, and I hopped in Tori's car. I cried the whole ride to her and Edge's home, but I made myself a promise that after today, I'd never cry for this man again.

Chapter Ten
TORI

I couldn't believe the shit Kilo had done but then again, he, Edge, and Drip were one and the same. They were fine fly ass niggas with money and big dicks who seemed to think they were God's gift to women. After giving Edge a dose of his own medicine, he has been on the straight and narrow, and I've been on my best behavior as well. My heart went out to Louve because I knew how much she loved Kilo. He and the kids were her entire world, so for him to crush her like this, after all the shit she stuck it out for with him was a slap in the face. My bestie had officially snapped and was out for blood with Kilo. I had to let her vent and get everything off her chest with no judgment like she had done for me on many occasions behind her brother.

I had to bring Louve to my house to calm her down and help her to relax. After a few too many glasses of wine and hours of tears and outburst, she was passed out in the theater room on one of the recliners. The family had been blowing both of our phones up, but Louve needed me, and we didn't need more stress added, so I text Ms. Lolly and Edge, and then silenced our phones. I busied myself with laundry and cleaning, but I really wanted to know who this Naomi chick was.

I logged into Facebook and started my search on her. I came across who I believed it to be, but when I looked further into the public pictures, I damn near lost my mind. This damn girl Naomi was saying R.I.P to her brother Saga on multiple photos. Was this really her brother or was it because of her ties to Fresh? This world was small as hell, and all my answers were confirmed. Not only was Saga her biological brother, but his partner Fresh was tagged in numerous photos as her man. This was all becoming too much, and I needed to call Egypt immediately. I dialed Egypt up and got no answer. I shot her a text to get back to me as soon as possible. I placed a call to this PI that I knew and gave them all the info I had on all the people I needed him to run checks on starting with Naomi and Fresh.

———

Egypt had got back to me right away, and she was just as worried as I was about all the shit that was going down. I had a gut feeling we had been set up and ambushed from all angles. This was all no coincidence, and Egypt agreed with me. Egypt hadn't told Drip about any of this, and that had me worried for their relationship. They worked through things and were now back together and on a secret trip that they refused to give details on. Egypt said they would be back in two days, and we would discuss things over lunch.

Edge text me that Kilo was up and pissed the fuck off that Louve tried to kill him while he was already in a coma. Kilo was threatening filing charges if Louve didn't come and talk like a grown woman with him. I told Edge to let Kilo know he had some damn nerves to be mad when he has a baby mama popping up out the blue on my girl at the damn hospi-tal. These men had taken us threw the damn ringer and had the nerves to be mad when we lose our cool and trip the hell out on them.

I let Louve get her much-needed rest and refused to bother her with his nonsense. Plus we had a bunch of more pressing shit to worry about than Kilo almost dying. The nigga was alive, so he better be thankful. Shit, Louve got his ass up out that coma, so he had better say thank you to her.

I was too impatient to keep sitting around waiting on my PI, so I decided to go out and do some snooping of my own. I left Louve a letter and was on my way. I needed to see what the hell was up with these people because I had a feeling that they were out for blood behind Saga and who knows what else, but I was going to get to the bottom of this shit. My first stop was the club where Naomi worked. I knew a few chicks there that I knew I could pay for some info, and I was about to do exactly that.

Drip

We had a few hours to kill before our flight left for Vegas, so I decided to pull up on Mama Alves and check her out. Egypt was dam near comatose from all the D I gave her last night into the early morning. I pulled into the driveway and shut the car off. I took in the sight of Egypt with her little belly in her fitted T-Shirt dress. She looked beautiful and I was happy as hell that we had made up. I tapped her leg to wake her up so we could go inside. She rubbed her eyes and smiled at me looking from me to the house. Mama Alves and Egypt were extremely close, and Mama Alves always had something good to eat so I knew that had to be the reason for her smile.

The screen door was closed and locked as usual, but the

main door was wide open letting out the delicious smelling aroma of the beef pot roast. I knew that smell and it was one of my favorite dishes that Mama Alves cooks and one she taught me to make as young boy. I knocked on the screen and waited for my beautiful lady to come around the corner and into the foyer but instead of her face I was met with Muse's mean mug. He smirked at Egypt and that shit rubbed me the wrong way. I hadn't expected to see my cousin, but it was good he was here because I had been needing to catch up with him.

He stepped out and held the door open for us. I gave E the head nod letting her know it was cool to head inside. I needed to discuss some things with Muse anyway and now was perfect since he seemed to be avoiding my calls.

"Yo, fam what's good I been hitting your line for a minute now" I said while sitting on the chair on the porch and pulling out my blunt to spark up. I puffed a few and passed it to Muse and he took it before he finally spoke.

"Man, I been moving how I do. Y'all good though out here. Y'all niggas names ringing bells y'all got shit on lock what you need with me?" He replied passing the blunt back and leaning up against the wall by the door.

His comment through me for a loop and I had studied his body language and he was standoffish as he never made eye contact with me. I shook my head and took a few puffs before putting my shit out and making my way inside to check on my two queens. I decided not to even respond to Muse because he was the same way when we were younger. Anytime I did some shit for me or on my own he would throw salt on me and whatever I was doing. When I first came to stay with Mama Alves he hated the love and atten-tion she was showing me.

It was clear he was on the same shit now that we were

grown as hell. He didn't like the fact that I went out on my own and did some shit without him and no help from him. He was running an operation that wasn't gone get us up out the hood and I needed to make moves for my family and myself. I was player chess not checkers and if I had to leave my hating ass cousin behind while I take this ride then so be it. I had my woman and a baby on the way to be concerned with. My brother Kilo was in a coma and we weren't the same without him out here bending corners and running shit with us. Right now, all I wanted to do was spend time with Mama Alves tell her my good news and then go marry my woman.

"Hey Mama, how you are doing?" I said as I entered the kitchen. I gave her a hug and she rubbed my face and then popped it lightly.

"Aww mama why you do that?" I asked backing away and grabbing a water out the fridge.

"Because I have been leaving your tail messages and you have not returned my calls. What is that about Dreon?" She replied turning back to the potatoes she was mashing up.

"I know and I'm sorry mama I been busy working" I replied taking a sit at the table. Just as Muse walked in and went to the living room.

"Yea from what Muse tells me you out here in some drug ring doing all types of reckless shit and we worried about you Dreon" She said turning to me giving me a stern look.

"Mama I'm good. I came here to tell you me and Egypt are having a baby" I changed the subject and in walked Muse looking pissed that grandma was now hugging me and Egypt with tears in her eyes.

"I am so happy for y'all I can't wait for this baby I am just so happy" She replied excitedly.

Muse smacked his teeth and stormed out the house and I just shook my head at the way he was acting. I let it be

because the important people were right here and other than
them no one else but my crew and the family mattered. I was
done rocking with Muse cousin or not he had jealous ass
tendencies and before I did some shit that I may regret I
would just cut him off.

To be alive was a blessing and I should be happy and embracing the fact that I'm up out that coma, but I'm far from that. I'm pissed the hell off that the reason I'm up out of that coma is because my damn woman tried to end my life. I had been trying to reach Louve for days, and she had her phone off. I haven't seen my kids, and I'm stressed the hell out. Louve has lost her damn mind if she thought her ass was about to disappear on me again, not this time. I'd do whatever the fuck I had to do because she was gone hear me out and talk about this shit.

Then I have Naomi ass popping up causing all this shit knowing damn well that isn't my baby. I told her ass to get rid of it just to be on the safe side, and this bitch took my threats lightly. I had the mind to send someone to find her ass, but I was going to handle her soon enough. This shit blows up in my face like a damn volcano the one time I decide to get my dick wet just a little. I had shit to handle, and Edge had a sit-down with Dons coming up to discuss the info he found out on Saga and let them know Saga has been handled. Although he told me he had shit under control, I needed to be there with him and have his back. It was only right.

Then we have Ms. Lolly and her bullshit. She lit into my ass after I was stable, and the doctors Okayed her to come in and see me. She hugged me tight and prayed over me before she cursed my ass out for the shit in that letter that Naomi left with Louve that sent her away again. She then told me everything about being my paternal grandmother and the true story of what happened with my father and mother. She showed me pictures I'd never seen of myself and my parents holding me when I was born. I was shocked but happy that I had family, and that I wasn't some motherless and fatherless kid no one wanted all along.

I explained to her that I had cut Naomi off, and she had to be lying about the baby, or it wasn't mine. I told her that when Louve left me, I cut Naomi off and had been focused on the kids business and getting Louve home where she belonged. Ms. Lolly wasn't trying to hear that shit though and told me I better fix this shit and fix it fast before Louve leaves my ass for good this time. I told her I planned to do just that as soon as I got out this damn hospital. She promised to bring my kids up to see me first thing in the morning, and I decided to start my investigating.

I hopped on Facebook as soon as Ms. Lolly left, but Louve had blocked my ass yet again. I would find her, and I knew I'd need help from my PI, so I shot him a text message.

———

It was quiet and dark as hell when I woke up and realized I wasn't alone. Edge set next to my bed in the recliner looking out the window. I sat up and cleared my throat to get his attention.

"My bad for waking you and being here this late, but we

got major issues, and I don't think you're safe, so I'm having you moved to private home with nurses and staff to look after you. The meeting and business with the Dons are off. Don Cortez ordered a hit on his own brothers by way of his secret son, and we stepped in, messed up his plan, and killed his son. The other two Dons have exiled him, and he is being held in a hole, but he has made it appear as if we were in on it too, so the Dons don't know who to trust and refused to sit down with me. I have the proof if they would listen and watch the recordings of what Saga said. Fuck! This shit is going from bad to worst quick as hell. So, with all this shit, I don't trust no one, and I feel like Don Cortez may have been the one to have you hit up, and I can't take any chance with them finding you here. I'm sending the whole family to a secret location until further notice," he said, sounding stressed as hell.

"Damn, well, you know I'm rocking with you. I'm always TTG and down for whatever. I'm recovering but a nigga not dead. As for Louve, you gone have to drag her ass to whatever hideaway you got because she for damn sho ain't trying to be nowhere right now with me. I still can't believe she tried to end my shit with no damn hesitation. They said the cords came out and my IV was snatched out so quick they had no clue what the hell was going on. Then she goes missing as if she ain't got some explaining to do about the shit she did. I swear to God Edge, if I ain't love her crazy ass and respect you, I'd been done hurt her a long time ago. Louve ass be getting away with a lot of bullshit, man." I shook my head running my hand down my face she had my ass stressed.

"Mannnn, I feel for yo ass because baby sis isn't nothing nice, and she's on a rampage now. That bitch Naomi done opened Pandora's Box, and I don't see that shit stopping any time soon. However, what I do know is her ass have no choice but to be in a house and in a room with you because she is taking her ass to the safe house no matter what she says. Shit, we all are going until shit gets handled. I got some shit lined up and some people in high places working on a few things, and once I get word shit that is all good we'll be back in Englewood and running shit how we supposed to," he replied, standing up and slapping me up.

"I hear you man, just make sure you check Louve before we get up there and she tries to take my ass out for real. I'm jive scared of her ass," I replied while laughing.

Edge laughed, shaking his head and then left out.

I was left to my thoughts, and I prayed that Louve would hear me out, and we could work on some issues while we were there before returning home. I planned to return home together and as an engaged couple and planning a wedding. Hopefully, cupid was on my side and helped a nigga out. I decided that I would bring the ring and depending on how things turned out, I would pop the question ASAP. As crazy as shit has gotten, I knew from the feeling in the pit of my stomach that I had to get my woman back. Even if she had tried to kill my ass, I knew I loved her beyond a doubt. With four kids, years put in, and everything possible to try to end us, it was time to lock her down.

Chapter Twelve

LOUVE

My resting bitch face was full display as I sat on a luxury-style tour bus that Edge ordered to ship all of us up to this safe house. I was beyond pissed off that he was ordering us to leave and stay at a secret location that we weren't even given information on. Everyone was on the bus except for Egypt and Drip who were still away on their impromptu getaway. According to Edge, we needed protection and around the clock security in order to remain safe, so this was how he had to do things. He refused to tell us why, and that further pissed me off. How do you tell me I have to go some damn where but refuse to tell me why or what the hell is going on?

Then forcing me into a space with Kilo knowing damn well we were on the outs was adding fuel to the fire. I couldn't even look at him, and I'm supposed to be in a house with him for who knows how long. They had me all types of fucked up if they thought I was about to play nice and be cool with his lying cheating ass. They could forget that shit. I had no nice words for Kilo, so if I were him, I'd steer clear of my ass if he knew what was best for his crippled ass. I was liable to pop off on this bus, and Edge knew that which is why he decided to sit up front blocking me from getting to the back of the bus where Kilo was resting with a private nurse accompanying him.

The kids were in their glory with their daddy back around, and as mad as I was, I was glad to see them happy, but I refused to let him see that. He looked good as hell too, which was pissing me off because I was beyond sexually frustrated, and my hormones were through the roof. Therapy must have been doing his ass some good, and Edge sent a barber to cut his hair before they left the hospital, so his ass was on point, and I was mad that I was turned on as soon as I laid eyes on him. He was walking with a walker and making strides maneuvering that around especially on the tour bus. I needed to take my mind off all this bullshit, so I powered on my Kindle and decided to read. I settled on Jae Tene's *Enticed by a Block Boy*.

———

After hours on the bus, we finally pulled up to this huge gated home. Everyone was glued to the windows in awe of the enormous place. Ms. Lolly rounded up the kids from the back of the bus with Kilo, and we all started to gather our bags and things to exit the bus. The gate opened, and the bus pulled into the turn style driveway. The home was like something off *MTV Cribs*. I was in shock at the size of this place. There were security guards lined in various areas and cameras on each point of the home. They weren't lying when they said we were on lock and fully protected around the clock.

The kids ran to the house and straight inside as we all took our time walking inside. I was almost in the door when I felt a sharp sting on the back of my arm. I dropped my bag and turned around quickly, ready to curse someone out to be met with Ms. Lolly and her mean mug. I rubbed my arm before speaking because the shit was on fire.

"Ms. Lolly, excuse my French, but why the hell did you pinch me? That shit hurts," I said, still wincing in pain.

"You say another swear word at me Miss Lady, and I'll do more than pinch that damn arm of yours. Now, you need to cut the bullshit out and talk to Kilondre, and that my dear is an order, neither a question nor suggestion. Y'all damn kids are working my nerves more than the real kids around here. Shit, now I'm cursing. Move out my damn way!" she shouted, stopping past me in her Jesus sandals and slamming the front door in my face.

I couldn't believe how her ass just acted.

"You better listen to her. She plays no games. She beat my ass yesterday with my own cane for telling her to mind her business," Kilo said behind me in my ear stepping up on me and purposely letting his stiff wood rub against my ass before stepping around me.

I didn't speak. Shit, I couldn't speak. I was trying to control my breathing, and the smell of his cologne had my mind betraying me as I envisioned myself in his arms making love and inhaling the smell of his cologne as I kissed his neck. I hadn't even realized my eyes were closed until I felt his lips on mine, and my eyes shot open. I couldn't resist as he tongued me down and then turned me loose and left me there as he made his way inside with a walker.

I was left stuck on stupid as the security guards just laughed at me. I turned around mean mugging them, and they quickly shut the laughing down and looked away. I stormed inside and to the back to see the kids playing on the swing set and in the treehouse. This was going to be a hard task trying to keep my distance from Kilo.

Chapter Thirteen

TORI

I slowly climbed out of bed, retrieved my laptop, and headed downstairs to handle some business. The house was pitch black and quiet as hell as I made my way along the long hall to the stairs. I used the light from my phone to look at the stairs as I walked down them. I entered the kitchen and flicked the switch on and damn near screamed, waking the whole house. Louve was seated at the table drinking what I assumed was tea and just staring at me as I stared at her weird acting ass.

"You scared the shit out of me, Lou. Why are you down here in the dark and alone at four in the morning?" I asked, pulling out a chair and sitting down across from her at the table.

"I'm stressed out, T. This shit with Kilo is heavy on my mind, and he kissed me earlier, throwing me completely off my square. I need space away, and Edge locking us all in this house isn't helping me. I was ready to let him bend me over on the spot with the way he had me feeling. Ugghhh, I just don't know what to do. Furthermore, Ms. Lolly done flipped on my ass, basically threatening me to talk to Kilo, and she was not even playing," Louve replied before taking a sip of her tea.

"Whewwww child, I ain't even gone get started on Ms. Lolly. I love her, but I'd be telling her old ass to mind her business, but that's just me. You know I don't give a damn. As for how you are feeling, don't be too hard on bro. I think he may have learned his lesson. After all, you did try to kill him, and he still loves your crazy ass. That's actually why I am up. I need to read up on the info that the PI sent me. I wouldn't be too concerned with that Naomi chick. I think it really was that one situation with them that happened, and he ended it, and now she trying to pin a baby on him. Let Egypt and me get the details on all this because she has some shit that involves the same people, and once we know, we will fill you in. In the meantime, hear my brother out and have that talk with him, boo. It's long overdue. Y'all never even discussed your first disappearing act because the shooting and car accident happen, and by the grace of God Kilo survived. Y'all owe each other and y'all kids the talk," I replied.

I hugged her, and she made her way upstairs with no other words spoken between us. I knew Louve, and she was going to handle things just as I suggested. It was only right and fair that they talked the very least, but I know it'll be a matter of time before they were lovebirds again.

I got on my laptop and began reading the notes on what info the PI was able to get, and I needed to show this shit to Egypt ASAP. I dialed her phone, and it went straight to voicemail, so I left a message telling her they needed to get their behinds back to Cali and to the safe house immediately. I hung worried that they possibly weren't safe being in out in the open wherever they were. I knew I should have been contacting Edge and telling him all the info that I had been given, but he was already stressed, and I felt it was my duty to take this matter into my own hands and get it handled.

I felt partly responsible, and the guilt was eating away at me. I had bedded the enemy unknowingly, and then I let my broken heart carry me on a revenge path that backfired and caused more bullshit than it was even worth. I was mad at myself for falling into that shit and doing the things I did. I was glad that Edge didn't kill my ass and had actually got his act together, which was what I wanted. However, this shit that was happening around us was tied up to the shit Saga and I did, and the fact that Edge erased Saga from the face of the earth, I knew his team and family was looking our way, and that was the reason shit was going up in smoke.

I was growing furious at the details of the plot that the PI discovered, and the snake that was the culprit behind it all was shocking and disappointing, but I had all I needed to put my own plot together, and I would get the last laugh. You could bet that shit for a fact. I closed up my laptop and went back upstairs to lay down with Edge, but to my surprise, he was wide-awake sitting up in the bed smoking with the TV down low as reruns of *A Different World* played.

I went to climb in the bed, but he pulled me over to him to straddle his lap. I looked down into his low eyes and knew he was lifted. I took the blunt from him and took a few puffs before passing it back. My mind was racing with the things that I had just found out, but I couldn't bring that to him yet, and I promised Egypt I'd keep her secret.

"What's on your mind, T? You look stressed out," he asked. He put the blunt out in the ashtray on the nightstand and lifted me off his lap. He laid me down, removing my robe, and started massaging my back.

"I'm just worried about you guys. We out here in the damn boonies, and you have yet to tell me what prompted this emergency stay at this safe house. We have security, but I can't even go out and shop, eat, drink, or nothing. I'm just concerned, Edge," I replied, sitting up on my knees and turning to face him.

We just stared at each other, and he looked more stressed than I did as I stared in his eyes. I wrapped my arms around his neck, and he looked down at my breasts as they set in his face in my purple lace Fenty bra. I knew what my man needed, and to be honest, I needed him to. I needed to take my mind off the pressing issues and just feel good.

No words were needed as I felt his hand reach up and unhook my bra with one swift motion. He pulled down one side slowly until it was off my arm freeing my breasts as I pulled my arm out the other one. I felt chills go up my back as goosebumps appeared as I anticipated his touch. He watched me like a lion watches its prey as he took my swollen nipples into his mouth one at a time alternating with each. I had already drenched the crotch of my thong, and I was beyond ready to feel him deep within me.

He gently pushed me back on the bed and trailed sensual kisses along my body. Edge was a thug ass nigga, but when it came to me, he gave me just enough of that soft, sensual loving along with that rough thugged out shit I craved. I let my man take my mind off the madness as he lapped circles in my wet center sending on an intense orgasmic wave that I knew was just the beginning of the many he sends me on.

Chapter Fourteen

KILO

I was up early before anyone else to work out with my personal trainer. We'd been cooped up in this house for a few weeks now, and Louve still hadn't budged in the way she was feeling. We talked about the kids, and that was about it. Her stomach was growing big, but that was all baby. She still had her perfect shape, and I was missing laying up with her the baby moving around. I was on a mission today to break down that wall she had up with me and get my woman back so that I could make her my wife. Louve had no idea I was able to move around now without my walker or cane. I had been putting on muscle with the help of my trainer.

I was sweating and ready for a shower after the workout I just had. I headed upstairs and decided to peek in on Louve. I turned the knob, and surprisingly, it wasn't locked. She was laid in the bed on her side with her ass tooted in the air in her nightgown. The bottom of her cheeks was hanging out and looked like they were waiting for me. I decided to let her rest and made my way to the shower in the wing of the house I was staying in. I showered, and all I could do was think of Louve and the way I missed her. I ain't have to jack my shit off in a long ass time, but I was gone have blue balls for real if I didn't get some soon.

I stepped out the shower wrapping the towel around me and making my way to my room. I entered the room and had to rub my eyes and make sure I wasn't seeing shit. Louve was sitting in the middle of the king-sized bed staring at me with that sex-crazed look on her face. I was skeptical about approaching her since we had yet to really talk, but I didn't even have to make the first move before she was off the bed and tonguing me down. My missile was ready for takeoff and at full attention underneath my towel. Louve wasted no time removing my towel and stroking my wood. I was in amazement that she was really in here handling me like this, but I guess when your hormones are out of whack you gone go for what you need and want.

We kissed hungrily and sloppily as we made our way to the bed. I wanted and needed to taste her honey. I laid her back, and she spread her legs, letting me see her bare cat dripping wet. The fact that she came ready for this into my room turned me on even more. I dove in face first like I hadn't had a meal in days. The sexy moans and the way that she was riding my face had me ready to go. I finally came up for air, and the words she was speaking was music to my ears.

"Put it in, daddy!" she moaned out as she played in her wetness waiting for me.

I ain't say a thing and did as I was asked. I placed the head at her opening and had to pace myself because of how tight and wet she was. Once I was all in, I held it in and kissed her biting and nibbling at her lip as she moved for me to make her cum.

———

I rubbed my eyes and tried to adjust them open, but the

sunlight was blinding me. I sat up, and flashbacks of the intense love Louve and me made last night put a smile on my face. I looked over on the right side of the bed, and it was empty. Louve fell asleep last night in my arms but was nowhere to be found now. I got up and went to use the bathroom and handle my hygiene before starting my day. I made my way downstairs, where I heard my kids laughing and chatting. I entered the kitchen, and Ms. Lolly and the kids were seated at the kitchen table playing Sorry and eating breakfast. I grabbed a few pieces of bacon and made my way to the wing of the house that Louve chose to alienate herself to.

I heard music playing and smelled the scent of candles, so I knew what time it was. Louve always lit her candles and soaked in a hot bath while playing her playlist. I stepped next to the bedroom door and listened closely.

"Go figure
You were the trigger
You brought me to an obstructed view
When you knew the picture was bigger
Who am I kiddin'?
Knew from the beginning
You'd ruin everything. You do it every time
You are my enemy. You are no friend of mine, muhfucker
Uh, you muhfuckin' right
You muhfuckin' right, I'm bitter
You muhfuckin' right, I'm triggered."

I be dammed, I thought we were good, and she is here listening to Jhene Aiko's crazy ass. I stepped into the room and made my way to master bathroom in her room. I stood in the doorway, watching her laid back with her bath pillow and bubbles piled high around and on her. She had her eyes closed as she sang along to the song. Louve had a decent voice, and she was singing her little heart out in here. I sat on the edge of the whirlpool tub just watching in awe of her. This was the woman for me, and I needed to do whatever was necessary to get her out her feelings and back on the same page with me.

"OH MY GOD KILO, you scared the shit out of me! Why are you sitting here just watching me and not announcing yourself like a weirdo?" she shrieked out.

"My bad, beautiful, I was enjoying the sound of your angelic voice, not feeling the song choice. I hope you ain't still trying to take your man out talking about being triggered and shit. You already tried to kill me once, so I think we even," I replied, giving her an once-over as she sat up and rolled her eyes at me.

The song had ended but started right back up, so I got up and cut the Beats Pill off completely, ending her concert session.

"Can you give me some privacy? Please I'd like to bathe in peace," she said, pulling the shower curtain closed, but it was no use because I snatched it back open.

"I think you have had enough alone time, and why the hell did you leave out the room with me? You could have taken a bath there, and I would have joined you," I replied while rubbing her foot that I had pulled out of the water and onto my lap.

"We fucked last night because I needed it, not because I was trying to make-up with you, Kilo. I still need some time to think about if I can move past all of this and your side baby," she said a little too easily and calm for me.

"What the hell you mean you just wanted to fuck? SO, YOU USED ME? WOW! Who the hell are you right now, ma?" I yelled, pushing her foot back in the water off my lap and jumping up, ready to punch a hole in the wall. I was hot as fish grease.

"Calm your ass down, and yes, I just needed some dick.

That's why I took my ass back to my own room once you passed out," she replied, shrugging her shoulders.

"Yo, you flaw as fuck for that shit, Lou. Using me as a fuck like we ain't got a whole family. You know what, keep your pregnant hormones out my bed, and I hope you enjoyed last night. It's the last time you get this dick. You are not about to be playing my ass like a lame ass nigga who doesn't love your cold-hearted ass. I don't even know who the hell you are right now!" I yelled, storming to the door.

I looked back at her once last time before shaking my head, and her ass started to cry as I stared at her. This shit was too much. This pregnancy had her ass evil as hell and emotional as fuck, and it was no way that I could keep up. I didn't know if I was coming or going right about now.

Chapter Fifteen

LOUVE

My emotions were out of freaking control, and I was losing my mind. I was weak and had broken down and had sex with Kilo. Who am I kidding we made love, and I felt it in my soul when we did. Kilo was my heart, and he had hurt me badly, but I believed that he was ready to make things right and focus on us. I had my mixed feelings, and my anger would resurface at the thought of that bitch Naomi, but my talk with Tori had me ready to hear him out. I guess these hormones were working against me because I soon didn't want to deal with him again just that quickly.

But seeing his reaction and hearing him just a few moments ago had me feeling like shit. I knew I loved that man and everything about him even after the bullshit, and I was trying to fight those feelings, but it was no use because now I'm all in my feelings, and those shits is hurt after how he looked at me and talked to me. I showered after I let the bathwater out and stepped out of the tub. I wrapped myself in the towel and headed to the room to change and have this talk with Kilo. I needed to apologize and also tell him to be patient with me and work with me, and that I am willing to do the same.

I dressed in a basic Fashion Nova t-shirt dress and some slides and headed to find Kilo. I kissed the kids each on their foreheads and asked Ms. Lolly where Kilo was. She told me he left with the security guard to get some fresh air. I was a bit disappointed, but I'd just wait on him to return later. I had ordered a bunch of art supplies and decided to go to the entertainment room and paint my frustrations out. I used my art as an outlet to release, and it was therapeutic and beneficial to me. Painting was calming and helped me gather my thoughts and really think on important things.

I had ended up painting over three pictures in one sitting and decided to call it a day. I made my way back to the living room to see if Kilo had returned and the kids were knocked out on the pallet they made watching movies in the family room. I checked the clock, and it was damn near eight in the evening, and the house was extremely quiet for all the people that stay here, which was odd. I searched the house and found Ms. Lolly in the study asleep on the chaise lounge with her crossword puzzle book on her lap.

I found Tori and Edge in the backyard in the hammock just chilling and passing a blunt between them. *Damn, I missed them type of nights.* I continued my search and still no Kilo. I noticed bags and shoes in the mudroom that wasn't there before and made my way to the last large room off the back of the house. I knocked at the door, and no one answered. I pushed it opened, and Egypt and Drip were passed out in the huge king platform bed. I smiled at the fact that they were back on track and had made it here safe and sound.

I closed the door and made my way to my room to lay down and watch TV. I entered my room, and my mouth dropped open in shock. Kilo was seated on the bed with a beautiful bouquet of pink roses, my favorite. He had candles lit and gift bags all around the room. I closed and locked the door and walked over to him. He stood handed me the roses and got down on one knee, causing my hands to start shaking, and the tears began to fall. I couldn't believe he was about to do this.

"Louve, I know I probably don't deserve another chance, but baby, I have to ask because after the way things have been, I know I need you in my life forever. When those bullets pierced me and my car went in the air, my life flashed before my eyes. However, the things that stood out the most when I saw flash were moments with you and our kids. Y'all are my lifeline and without y'all it's no purpose for me. I ain't have the family life growing up, and I spent a lot of days alone in this world just do whatever to survive, but the day I met you, and we got together my world been better. You gave me the care, support, and love I needed when I didn't even know I was missing it. You made my days brighter and my nights complete. You have blessed me with the precious gift any woman can give a man, and that's birthing their children, but most importantly, you have raised my kids and been the best mother to them, and I value that more than you know. I love you Louve will you please Marry me, baby?" he said, wiping the few tears I had off my face.

"Yes, Kilo, I will marry you," I said between sobs.

He placed the most beautiful pink diamond ring on my finger, and we kissed. I knew in his arms at that moment I was with my soul mate, and I was rocking until the casket dropped and in the next life. He was mine, and I was his. The talk was no longer necessary. I was just ready to make love to my man and wake up in his arms this time. I wanted to start planning our wedding and continue to wait for our next bundle of joy to arrive, but you know how the universe is, you get a window of happiness and then here come the clouds of bullshit to rain on the parade.

Chapter Sixteen

EDGE

I was finally able to get away from Tori so that I could handle this business. Tori had become extra clingy over the last few weeks, and I could never get away without her on my ass about where I was going and what I was up to. Today I paid for a spa service to come out and give the ladies spa treatments at the safe house. Kilo was adamant about coming along, but I slid out on him with Drip because he wasn't 100% how he said he was. He was still limping around trying to carry on like he didn't need to still rest and recover.

We were riding to the home that Don Cortez was being held in. The heads of the families and the other Dons were determining Don Cortez's fate soon. Don Cortez was a rat and a snake, and he tried to flip that shit on us now that Saga was dead and gone. Saga was his son that the Dons and families knew as a friend of his kid he took in. He had plans to take the families, and Dons out and have Saga and his crew help him run everything. Me killing Saga ended his plan and sent him running to the Don's with lies to take us out.

The Don's already had their suspicions about Don Cortez, but family is first, so they shut us down and cease all business and contact until they had all answers, but I had that all covered for them. I had all the evidence and proof, and with Don Cortez dead, the issue was removed. All I had to do was get in a meeting to provide them with all the facts of what Don Cortez was actually up to. I was basically doing them a favor for free that was beneficial to us all. I only needed a seat at the table to get the type of bread they were getting.

We were all riding in silence lost in our thoughts in the van disguised as a plumbing van all dressed as plumbers. Drip was quiet but was ready to go war, and that's exactly what I needed. We had some of our young bulls from the crew with us, the security guard, and our driver. We pulled up to a large home on a hill behind a massive tall gate. The driver was the brother of one of the guards that were guarding Don Cortez. We had non-detectable medicine that would be injected into him. I wanted to shoot his in his face, but that was too risky, so we had to make it look like a natural heart attack. Once word got back that he was dead, we'd pay our respects send condolences and set up that meeting to discuss the lies he has told.

The driver used the badge supplied to him and entered around back in the fake plumbing truck that we rode in. We pulled in, and after flashing our fake badges, we were let into the home. We were taken to the opposite side that Don Cortez was on, and once the man escorting us turned his back, we knocked him out and placed him in a chair in an office off to the side.

We split up and hit all four corners. Drip and I had the back area where Don Cortez was locked up at. We reached the room and the guard went walking by us, giving us a head nod that we were good to go in. We entered, and Don Cortez was laid on his stomach with headphones in as he slept chained to the bed. I approached him with the needle ready. I jabbed it in his neck and pushed all the fluid in. He struggled to get up, but eventually, started to have a seizure and then just went out.

We backed away and walked out of the room, and the guard was coming back, sipping a cup of coffee. He nodded and set back in his spot outside the room. We met back up with the guys and made our way to the truck. We were on our way back home to wait for the rest of the pieces to fall into place. I needed a drink and a blunt and to be up in my woman to ease my stress while I waited for Don Cortez's death to be hot news on the streets. I was hoping that over these last few weeks I'd knocked Tori up because I purposely kept her high and drunk and forgetting about them birth control pills so that we could finally have a baby.

Tori was gone kick my ass when she realizes what I been up to, but I ain't have no choice but to sneak my chance in. She was dead set on being married first, whereas I wanted our child to be there at the wedding. It was the same result in the end — a family together. All these niggas was having kids. Even one of my young niggas had a baby on the way, and here I was still kid-less. Nah that shit was a dub. I was about to get my seed even if I had to do it the trap star way.

Chapter Seventeen

EGYPT

I was loving life nowadays, and no shit could take me off my cloud. Even the shit we were about to do had me floating. I had married my best friend and was expecting our first baby. What more could a girl ask for? Drip was so attentive and much more connected with me, and I was falling more in love with him every day. I was hoping we hurried this shit up before the guys got home and beat our asses. Drip and Edge were out of town until the morning, but Kilo was just at physical therapy and would be back to the house soon.

We were on a mission to catch this Naomi bitch and get her ass for the shit she was pulling. Now, we weren't dumb. We took security with us and made sure to tell him some sob story for the pregnant women to get his sympathy. He was currently driving us to Naomi's condo, located in LA. I had all the dirt I needed, and this bitch was gone stop fucking with our family today. The fact that she was sent to approach Kilo and was working with Kelli to start shit all because they were following the orders of some bitter hating ass men was mind boggling.

Jay, the security guard, let us out in the front of the

boutique and apartment building, and we went inside with him following behind us.

"You know what ladies, I'm a sit right out here in the truck and wait on y'all because I can tell y'all gone take all day in here shopping. I see they passing out cocktails and appetizers and shit," he said before turning around and heading right back to the truck.

We didn't say a word. We nodded, smiled, and waited until he was in the truck before we headed to the back where the entrance from the apartment building was. The building connected and had an opening for residents to go in and not have to leave and go outside to enter. We made our way quickly to the stairwell and up the stairs. By the time we reached the fifth floor, we were all looking like that girl in the meme with the pink blazer on that was bent over squinting and out of breath. We were out of shape, and it was showing.

I opened the door and quickly shut it back and told the girls to be quiet. I could see Fresh outside of Naomi's apartment door, and she was trying to get the door opened. They appeared to be arguing, and he kept mushing her in the back of her head as she fumbled with the keys. Finally, they went inside, and I pulled out my chrome gold gun and proceeded to the door before Louve snatched me back.

"Bitch, where the hell you get a gun and do you even know how to use it?" she asked with a high-pitched voice.

"I've been shooting since I was 16 Lou Lou, and I have done some shit you not aware of that we can discuss later, but right now, we need to let these two idiots know we are on to them, and they are not getting away with this shit. Just follow my lead," I said, opening the door with them following behind me.

I slowly approached the door and listened closely. I could hear them arguing and yelling about her pregnancy. It started to get farther away, so I assumed they walked to the back. I was prepared to pop the lock with my tools, but I turned the knob, and the door came open. I pushed the door open slowly, and the girls stood in the hall looking from me to each other. I signaled for them to come on in. I reached in my bag and handed Louve a small gun, and Tori pulled her own out the small of her back. Louve's eyes grew wide as saucers as she realized we both were trained-to-go no holds barred.

"I don't know who the hell y'all are right now," Louve whispered.

We didn't speak another word as we headed down the hallway, passing the empty living room and kitchen combo. We could hear the shower running and what sounded like sobbing. I put my back to the wall and slid down the wall to the bathroom door. I used the crack to look in the medicine cabinet mirror, and I saw Fresh choking Naomi while holding her head under the shower water. He finally pulled her up, and she gasped for air and cried.

"Silly ass bitch, I gave you one job. Get in, get info, and kill his ass, and you fall in love and get dick silly. Then you are telling this nigga my seed is his. What the fuck is wrong with you, Naomi? I ain't break my foot off in yo ass in a minute because you are pregnant, but don't forget who the fuck I am!" he yelled, shoving her to the ground.

He pulled his pants down and pissed on her and in the process, he obviously didn't realize he left his gun on top of the toilet seat because as he held his eyes closed and head back, she grabbed the gun and shot him in the chest. He lunged for her, and she shot again until his body fell forward into the tub. She jumped out the way in time so that he didn't fall on top of her. Louve was shaking and holding her mouth in horror, but I was locked and loaded, and I knew we couldn't let her ass go. We had to kill her. It was no way around it. She started pacing and crying, and before I knew it, she had snatched the door open and screamed.

POP! POP! POP!

The bullets rang out quick as hell, and I had no clue who shot her as her head exploded and splattered around the bathroom. Her body fell on top of Fresh's, and I turned around to see Tori staring at Louve, holding the smoking gun with a crazed look on her face. I took the gun from her hand and sent Tori to lock the door. I then grabbed my Louve's purse and found her phone. I had to call Kilo because Drip would kill me, and since he and Edge were out of town on business, Kilo was our only hope to get this shit storm to disappear.

I called Kilo and ran what I could in code to him over the phone, and he said he would send help. He told us to leave the door to unlock and leave out the back door and walk around to the truck with security, and everything else would be handled. We hurried and did as he told us and made our way downstairs and out the back and walked around to the front. We hopped in the truck, and no words were spoken as JP the security guard, shook his head at us, and pulled off into traffic. I assumed that Kilo told him what happened, and he was disappointed that we would do that reckless shit, but oh well. What was done is done, and I refused to have these people out here gunning for our family any longer. There was one key player in this that I would have to reveal to Kilo Drip and Edge immediately.

This shit was gone kill them, and I know Drip especially was going to be hurt and probably pissed at me, but after I told the whole story and finally shared who I was before I met him, he would understand. I was stressed and wished that I could have a drink right now. I looked in the back at Louve who was staring out the window, and she turned and winked at me before looking back out the window. I looked at Tori, and she was just as lost as I was. Louve was acting crazy as hell, and I was wondered that she was either on the brink of a mental breakdown or was already having one.

"Don't worry. I ain't lost my mind. I found myself, and I'd say I just bossed the fuck up," she said, shocking the hell out me. I just turned my ass back around and put shades on. I needed a nap after today's events.

Chapter Eighteen

KILO

I couldn't believe when Egypt called me speaking in the code that Drip and I used to use back when we were running with Muse. Her ass basically killed two damn people and needed a cleanup crew ASAP. I had no clue what the hell her, Tori, and Louve ass was up to, but I was damn sure about to find the fuck out. I had to call in a favor to Muse for some backup, and I told him to slide through the hideaway to meet up and discuss things, and I'd slide him some paper for the cleanup job.

It was nearing eight in the evening, and the kids were winding down, so I left them in the theater room and made my way to wait in the study for the ladies to return. I directed security to bring them straight to the study to meet with me once they arrived back. I hadn't drunk in a long time, but I poured me a glass of Henny on the rocks and sipped it while I waited. I heard the car pulling up, and I decided to let them be escorted inside to me.

I could hear the girls going off on all the guards that were dragging them into the study. I cleared my throat at all the noise they were making, and they all shut up and looked at me as if they were shocked to see me sitting and waiting.

"I got them from here, fellas. JP, stand outside this door and let no one in or out until I say so," I stated, sipping the last of my drink.

"Ladies have a seat. Don't look so scared. After all, you all did just kill some people, right? Y'all out here catching bodies, now right? No one got shit to say?" I said, leaning forward and resting my hands locked into each other on the desk as I look at each one of them in the eyes. No one had yet to utter a word.

"Listen, Kilo. This shit was necessary. I have some shit to tell you, but I need Drip and Edge here so that I can say it all at once to everyone and not have to repeat myself," Egypt said finally speaking up as her other two goons stayed quiet.

I looked at her trying to figure out what the hell was up, but I was drawing a blank. I then looked at Louve, and she seemed relaxed and cool. Tori seemed a bit on edge and antsy, and I was starting to think that we might have a big problem on our hands.

"What y'all will do is tell me who the fuck y'all killed and why, and we will tell Drip and Edge everything when they return," I stated.

"We killed your side bitch after she killed her man and real baby daddy," Louve replied nonchalantly.

"WHAT THE FUCK DID YOU SAY?" I yelled, jumping up and walking over to where she was seated on the other side of the table by the window.

"YOU HEARD WHAT THE FUCK I SAID. SHE HAS BEEN HANDLED AND WILL NO LONGER BE AN ISSUE. NOW YOU CAN LEARN TO KEEP MY DICK IN YOUR PANTS, AND I WON'T HAVE TO GET OUT OF CHARACTER AND KILL CRAZY ASS BITCHES

THAT FALL IN LOVE WITH MY DICK!" she yelled, jumping up in my face.

I had no words because I was torn between pissed the fuck off and turned the fuck on. Louve was always sexy, but when she was mad, she had this fire in her. That sit turned me on, and the way she was talking had me ready to give her ass some act right, but we had company, so I just shook my head and went back to sit down. I needed another drink. I sipped and listened as they told me everything from the beginning and by the time they were done, I had to call in reinforcement as well as put security on alert not to let Muse in the gate. Muse was the snake all along that had me hit up and sent everyone that was against us our way.

He never wanted to get money with Edge because he wanted the position Edge held for himself. Muse had linked up with Saga and Don Cortez to take us all down for the opportunity to take Edge's spot once Don Cortez had all the territory to his self. With Saga gone, they were all falling apart and unable to carry the plan out as needed. I was beyond pissed because I'd just given our location to Muse unknowingly that he was against us and was the one who shot my car up and then ran it off the road. I always looked as Muse as family, but lately, he'd distanced himself from us, and I now knew why.

I let the ladies know that they need to stay in the boss bitch mode they were on because Muse now knew where we all were, and shit could get heavy at any minute around here. I texted Drip and Edge to get here 911 and prayed they weren't out on no mission, but something told me that they were out doing exactly that without me. I sent the ladies out except for Louve because we needed to talk. I had a surprise for her coming tomorrow, and I needed to make sure she was good because for her to have caught her first body. She was too calm for me.

"So, you catch your first body and just a straight gangsta now, huh?" I asked, pulling her in between my legs as I kissed her belly.

"I caught my first body, and I ain't scared to catch another one. Little green ass Louve is gone, and I'm the boss bitch behind her boss ass man," she replied, straddling my lap. I had no come back for that, but my dick was at attention and ready. If she weren't already pregnant, I know she'd be getting her club shot up tonight.

Chapter Nineteen

EDGE

I had received Kilo's messages, and we were already in the car heading back to the house. It was damn near two a.m. by the time we made it back home, but we were here, and I was ready to lay it down. However, we had a rude awakening the minute we pulled on the block of the safe house. We saw a figure tampering with the power box connected to the security gate. We shut the lights off and headed up the hill. I had the driver stop and let us out. Drip pulled out his piece, and I grabbed mine. We let security head around to the other side to ambush the culprit from within.

I forgot to grab my silencer, so I pulled an old school military move and crawled through the grass and bushes staying low. Drip followed suit and did the same and we pounced on that motherfucker. I swung the butt of my gun down on the nigga's head, and he dropped out cold in the lawn. I signaled security, and they opened the gate as we dragged the body into the guesthouse. Once we were inside, I flicked the light on, and Drip snatched the ski mask off revealing his cousin Muse.

"Yo, what the fuck?" Drip said, looking at his cousin in shock.

Muse was still knocked out cold, so I took it upon myself to place him in the computer chair, and zip-tied his hands to the armrests and tied his legs to the bottom of the chair. I called Kilo and told him to meet us in the guesthouse and don't let the ladies know where he was going but to hurry here ASAP. I was keeping my cool, but I was ready to off this nigga with no questions asked, but out of respect for Drip, since it is his cousin, I decided to wait on Kilo.

I looked up and instantly became upset as I saw the ladies and Kilo make their way into the guesthouse. The girls didn't seem shocked or alarmed that we were in here with Muse tied up and out cold. I just shook my head and put my gun back in the waist of my jeans.

"Yo, Kilo, what the fuck man? I specifically said don't tell the ladies and not bring they asses up in here!" I spat pissed the hell off.

"Chill out, Edge. The ladies have some shit to tell y'all, and it involves Muse and some shit they took upon themselves to go out and handle yesterday afternoon," he replied, leaning up against the wall and crossing his arms giving the ladies the floor to speak.

We all listened as Egypt explained everything to us from the very beginning all the way until the reason of why we can't trust Muse. Drip had veins pulsating out his neck as he stared at Egypt. I got up and stood closer to them just in case he lost his cool up in here on his pregnant wife. I was shocked at all the bombs they dropped on us, but everything now was crystal clear and made perfect sense. I knew for a fact we ain't have too many enemies out here, and the way shit was popping off, let me know that it was close to home and personal, but I never expected it to be this close to home for us all.

Then my baby sister out is here killing side bitches, and she doesn't seem the least bit fazed by that shit. I have no clue who the hell she is right now. I knew Tori had that shit in her. She's been rocking with my crazy ass long enough to have my shit rub off on her a little, so it was no shocker that she dug up info and handled that shit like a true ride or die bitch. My fiancée bossed the fuck up and held shit down in my place, and I commended her for that. With the shit that we're into and the life we live, ain't all glitter and gold. The shit gets rough and dirty. I was glad to have a thorough ass chick on my side. That shit was rare this day and age.

"So y'all out here bussing guns and shit. What y'all a think y'all some girl gang or some shit?" I asked, laughing but dead ass serious.

"Naw, we just down to ride for some real hittas," Louve said, leaning into Kilo as he wrapped his arms around her.

"Man, I don't know what the hell got into all y'all females, but y'all can let that shit go immediately. Y'all are not about to be out here on shit in these fucking streets. Thank y'all for the work y'all put in yesterday. Even though it was behind our backs, y'all came through and had our backs and that ain't unnoticed, but that shit stops here," I stated seriously to them.

"Why you never told me all this shit, Egypt? We fucking said no more lies and secrets when I changed your fucking last name E, so what the hell is all this shit about? Who the fuck are you? All this time you were being blackmailed by my cousin for some nigga he helped you kill that you owed money to, but come to find out, he played your ass and never really killed him. He just helped get you away from him and out here. So, fresh is your ex and you see this nigga out in Mexico while we there and you never told me shit? After all this damn time, this is how I get the truth?" Drip spat through gritted teeth.

I saw the look of fear on Egypt's face and decided to try to calm this shit down.

"Yo, Drip chill out and take it easy on your PREGNANT WIFE. She made some mistakes and was obviously scared for her life, so let's move past this shit, and decide what the fuck we gone do about your snake ass cousin," I said.

"Man, fuck that nigga! He ain't no kin to me. You can off that bitch ass nigga," he said then walked out the door.

Egypt followed behind him quickly, and we all just sat there looking stumped. I knew this nigga would be waking up sooner than later, so we had to figure some shit out and quick.

"Alright, I say let's pin everything back on him including Saga, Fresh, and Naomi's death and let the Dons handle killing him. When we deliver him to them, they will offer to compensate us, and that will then give me the ball in my court to get us put on in place of Don Cortez. It could be a long shot, but at this point, we don't have shit to lose, and we still got our operation, so we can open shop back up now," I suggested and waited as they all thought it over.

"Bro, that sounds like a good ass plan. Let's get us cleared, get the Dons off our radar, and eliminate this snake ass nigga in the process. Two birds one stone, let's do this shit," Kilo replied, slapping me up.

The plan was set, so I had security load that clown into the trunk of the truck and placed my call to the Dons. They agreed to accept my meeting and receive the important person I was bringing to them. I hope this shit went as planned. It's been niggas who made it to meetings with the Dons but never made it out and was never seen or heard from again.

Chapter Twenty

DRIP

Talk about .38 hot, man I was hotter than a motherfucker at Egypt. We just came back from getting married in Vegas, and she still had secrets and skeletons in her closet. She had more than ample opportunity to tell me what the fuck was up. I mean I met her through Muse, but according to them, all those years ago she was just a lookout for Muse, and once I snatched her up, that shit got shut down. I always felt like Muse was jealous of the relationship that I had with Egypt, but I never knew the shit went that deep. I had questions, and she was about to answer them shits tonight.

"You got anything other secrets, Egypt? Because I asked your lying ass that last time and you withheld the info about Muse, so what's the deal? Did you fuck my cousin?" I said, pulling a chair out from the table and sitting down in it, leaning forward so that we were face to face. She looked like she was on the verge of tears, but them salty ass tears ain't mean a thing to me. She was to blame for this shit.

"NO, Dreon, I never slept with Muse. He wanted to and tried, but I never went there with him. Once you and I became a thing, he started threatening to turn me into the police for killing Fresh. Muse told me he buried his body, and he had my gun with my fingerprints, so I started paying him. That's why I worked so hard to always have money so that I could keep him paid and still be successful. I never knew he was the one that came after Kilo and the family until a few weeks ago when Tori's P.I. discovered his ties to Saga, Naomi, and the Dons. I was scared, and I am so sorry, baby. Please forgive me," she cried as she pleaded with me to forgive her.

She reached for my face, but I slapped her hand away. I didn't know what to do at the moment, so I got up and left her in the kitchen and made my way out back to smoke and clear my head. I heard her call my name, but I needed to cool off before I said some shit I might regret. I sat by the pool and just smoked on this fat ass L I had rolled up. I felt someone close, so I turned to see Kilo taking a seat next to me. I offered him the blunt, but he pointed at his wounds and shook his head, declining the L.

"My bad, bro, fuck with everything that's going on, my ass forgot you still healing. Don't push it and end up back in that hospital, Killa Kilo," I said, looking back at the kitchen window where Egypt was staring at us with tears running down her face.

"You better tread lightly, bro. The hormones and emotions sis got going on is nothing to play with. Pregnant women can be evil as hell. You see, Louve tried to cancel my ass out of here," he stated while shaking his head.

"Man, these damn women are a trip. I wanted to knock Egypt head off after hearing that shit. This nigga Muse is a fuckin' fraud. Like, he's my own flesh and blood raised by our grandma under the same roof. Nevertheless, I always knew that nigga was jealous of me even as kids, but I brushed it off. The nigga was like a brother to me, but as of today he is dead," I said taking another pull of the Kush.

"Man, this shit is crazy. It'll be your own ones against you.

I know that shit hurts, and to be honest, the shit is fucking with me too because Muse brought me on and fucked with me the long way. However, greed and jealousy allowed him to gun for me, and I can never overlook or brush that off. It's on you, and if you can't end that fuck nigga, I'm a do it. Just say the word," he replied, dapping me up and getting up to go inside.

"Talk that shit out with your wife. Kiss and make up. Y'all two were made for each other. Happy wife happy life, my nigga," Kilo said before disappearing into the house.

I finished off my L and went to find my wife. I knew I wasn't leaving her, but that shit was fucking with me that she never came to me. As a man, we protect and provide, and if you can't come to me to protect you, then I failed you as your man. This Muse shit would have been handled from day one when she became mine.

I entered the room and heard the shower running in the bathroom of the room we were occupying. I entered the bathroom, and Egypt was under the shower letting the water cascade all down her body. Her round belly and swollen breasts looked like a work of art.

I still felt a way, but my heart softened at the sight of her. She was the yin to my yang. She calmed the savage within me, and after all the bullshit, my heart was still hers. After we said I do, I meant that shit forever. I came out of my clothes and pulled the shower door open. We locked eyes, and no words were even needed because we knew exactly what the deal was. I stepped into the shower fully and pulled her into me. Our naked bodies against each other and the water streaming down our bodies from the waterfall showerhead created a sexy feeling.

We kissed deeply, and she kept saying sorry in between each kiss. I didn't need any more apologies though. I needed her and needed to feel her in every sense of the way. Egypt was the only woman I ever made love to, and although we had dope ass quickies and fuck sessions, the love we made fed my soul and love for her every time. That love shit was always corny to me back in the day, but with Egypt, it's all I wanted and all that mattered to me. I loved her, and she loved me. Nowadays that's exactly what we men need in our crazy ass worlds. The love of a woman will have you feeling like the king of the world.

Chapter Twenty-One

LOUVE

The men were on their way to meet with the Dons, and we were ordered to keep our asses in the house. I was perfectly fine with that though, but now the other two were in full brat mode. I played board games with the kids while Egypt watched *Basketball Wives*. Tori was in the kitchen with Ms. Lolly whipping up a good ass dinner that I couldn't wait to be done. I got up to go pee, and the doorbell rang startling all of us. I looked back at everyone in the living room and into the open kitchen at Tori and Ms. Lolly.

"Gone get the door, girl. It's fine. With all that security out there, its safe child," Ms. Lolly said, turning back to the stove.

I stayed still a few more seconds, and then the bell rang again, so I made my way to it. I looked out the peephole and saw JP the security guard, so I opened the door. He stepped aside, and my mouth dropped. The tears fell fast as I stared at my father and mother holding hands and smiling wide at me. I was frozen speechless and couldn't move, then they both charged me with hugs and kisses, and I hugged them back crying like a baby.

I had both my parents here in the flesh, and my mother looked healthy and well. The most noticeable thing about her was the smile on her face, and the way she beamed with happiness. I pulled them in and introduced them to everyone and the kids. Today was the absolute best day of my life, and I couldn't wait for Edge to get home and see them. The last time we had both our parents, we were still kids, so this was a monumental moment for our family. I finally felt complete and whole, and that was the feeling I was yearning for and missing all this time.

The kids were so happy to have their grandparents, and they were talking them to death.

The kids and my parents went to the backyard to enjoy some more time alone, and I just watched from the kitchen window. I prayed things stayed on the up and up, and I prayed that the guys made it back to us safe and sound. The last thing we need is anything to happen to them. Tori and my mama hit off like old times, and she was happy to know that Edge was engaged to Tori. My dad was delighted as well and asked her when they planned to have some babies, and we all laughed because she was adamant about taking her time on that.

They were excited to be home and be here for the baby that I was currently carrying and for Egypt as well. With all that Egypt had been through in her life, all she had was Drip's granny and us since hers died a while back. Egypt was like a sister to Tori and me, and us three had each other for life.

Ms. Lolly threw down on dinner, and we all had seconds plus the peach cobbler cheesecake, which she made from scratch for dessert.

I told my parents the plans I had for a huge wedding pregnant and all and the business ventures I wanted to do. My mother was so excited, and she offered to help plan everything.

"I fell off once before baby girl, but now that I am clean and better, I vow to be a better wife, mother, and most importantly, a Glam-Ma to my grandkids. And yes, I said Glam-Ma because I look damn good and young as hell to be a grandma. I am so proud of the woman you turned into, and the man your brother is, and I'm going to do everything to make up what I did to you all. I have a second chance with my family, and I'm a make the most of that," my mother said, hugging me tightly.

I hugged her back as we shared in happy tears. There wasn't a dry in the house, and even my dad was misty-eyed even though he tried to play it off.

"Daddy, it's ok to have a good cry. Don't try to hide it," I said, kissing his cheek.

"Yo daddy's an OG. I don't cry, baby girl," he said, fighting back his tears. We all laughed as he walked down the hall to the bathroom to wipe his tears.

Everyone settled down throughout the house, and my parents took the guesthouse to have some alone time. Since being picked up at the airport by security, they hadn't been able to make up for the lost time, and that was TMI for me, so I let them go and went to shower and wait up for Kilo. I was floating on a cloud the whole way to my room as I thought about today. I couldn't wait to have my man home so that I could love on him properly. We had no more drama. It was just us, the kids, and to plan our wedding, and then we could wait for the arrival of our little one.

Chapter Twenty-Two

EDGE

We stood outside a vault-like door awaiting entrance to the meeting with the Dons. I'd be a lying motherfucker if I said I wasn't a little nervous. This whole thing had my ass off my square because I don't know what the hell we were walking into. I looked behind me as my guards stood behind us, waiting patiently as well. JP held the large sack we needed for this meeting to go as planned. I looked to Kilo on my right and Drip to my left, and although I wasn't much of a praying man, I shot a quick one up that our family back home would be protected.

The doors slid open, we were patted down, and all our guns were taken. They peeked in the sack and looked at us like we were crazy. I just shrugged my shoulders as they let us go by. We walked down a dim-lit tunnel behind a tall big Mexican nigga. He led us in a door and slammed it behind us. In front of us were six men sitting at a table lined up like a panel. I stepped forward, but a short man stood and put his hand up, stopping me.

"Why was it imperative for you to meet with us, Edge?" he asked with a cigar hanging in between his lips.

"I have something you may want, and proof of the deal Don Cortez was making behind all of your backs trying to take down the organization and keep it for himself and Saga, his secret child," I stated stepping forward placing the iPad on the table. I pressed play, and the videos began to play. Images, documents, and voice clips all played one by one confirming what I said. They all sat quietly, and the small one spoke up again.

"What is in the sack?" he said, lighting the cigar and walking around the table to where we stood a few feet away.

I signaled JP to bring the sack forward. He walked forward dragging the sack like it weighed nothing to him, and he untied and then lifted it, and Muse came rolling out hogtied and with his mouth taped.

The short man roared in laughter, and the rest followed suit. We weren't amused. It was but whatever at this point. I just wanted to know we were no longer targets and see what he offered us in exchange. Once the laughter died down, I told them everything that occurred, and that Muse was a part of it all and behind everything. They huddled up and talked for a few minutes before the short who I assume was in charge came back over.

"Kill him right now and prove your loyalty and alliance with our organization, and we will give you the original plan we had in place but will be making you the man in charge of the whole U.S. distribution and operation," he said leaning against the table puffing away on his cigar and looking at us for an answer.

Before I could even step up to take the gun, their guard brought forward Drip. He quickly fired a shot directly between Muse's eyes and one to his heart. His cries went unheard prior to the bullets piercing him due to the duct tape. They all clapped and two suitcases each were brought over to us. We picked up the suitcases and turned to make our way out.

"You are in now, and there is no option to turn away now. Welcome to the family," the short man said.

I wanted to know who was who, but I was confident they never stated on purpose. They wanted to keep it that way for good reason. These men were powerful and wealthy, so they had to stay ten steps ahead of everyone around them.

We all nodded our heads and walked out. Once in the car, we finally started slapping each other up because we were on in the biggest way we could ever be. Life was good before, but life now would be great. We discussed the details of who would be running what and thinking of all the niggas we were supplying throughout the U.S. that we needed to promote and pull into our shit. This was the way you flipped shit and took over the spot you never thought you'd get. I was ready to get shit rocking, and now our families could go the hell back home where we belonged.

———

I couldn't sleep after the meeting was over, I was still on a cloud, so I sat in the den and had me a few drinks. Everyone was already in their rooms, and we decided to head back to our own homes tomorrow. I heard what sounded like arguing, so I made my way out the den to see what was going on. I entered the kitchen, and my parents were engrossed in a stare down. My father was looking like he was fuming.

"Yo, what is going on in here? Y'all should be laid up making up for lost time, not arguing. What is the argument anyway?" I asked sitting on a stool at the island.

"Your mother is in here tripping because I reached out to some old associates who owe me money, and she is assuming that I'm jumping back into the game. Which if I decided to, I am the man of the house and head of this family I have the final damn say," my father replied, slamming a can of beer down on the counter.

"YOU know what, fuck it! Go on back out there and choose the life that contributed to my downhill spiral. You were never home, and I battled with the pain pills, and eventually, found something stronger to ease the pain. Maybe Ed, just maybe, if I had you there and your support like I needed, I wouldn't have failed y'all, so forgive me for wanting to keep you out of jail and here to be my rock, so I never fail y'all again," my mother cried.

"Damn Loucille, I never knew that shit. Why you never came to me?" my father replied, pulling my mama in for a hug.

"I tried Ed, but your head was so far in the game, you never stopped to listen to me. I tried for a long time to talk with you, baby. I'm sorry." My mother had broken down into a sob.

"Man, mama, I am so sorry for my behavior. I have held you at arm's length all this time even after completing rehab because I was still holding onto my feelings from childhood. You didn't have a support system, and I apologize for not hearing you out before. And pops, it doesn't mean that I fault you because you were just trying to provide for your family, so I get it and we all here now and we have the opportunity to make this family what it was always supposed to be," I said.

My mother broke from my father and hugged me tightly. I felt all the love that I tried to block out before in her arms, and I was happy as hell. I had my mother, my father, my sister, and a dope ass woman in my life. I know I had done some shit in my life, and we had gone through a tough ass time, but here we are together, and the shit felt good. Most people will say they don't need a mother or a father, but having both leave at crucial points in my life, I felt the repercussions of that, and I never want to know what it's like not to have them. My children will never know what it's like not to have both of their parents', God willing.

Chapter Twenty-Three

TORI

Four Months Later

I rode in the back with Egypt as Louve rode shotgun with Mama Loucille in the front as we drove to the strip club to crash our men's party. I was a little over four months pregnant with Egypt being six months, and Louve had my nephew early two months ago. Kore Zion Jones was a fighter and was still in the NICU, but getting stronger day by day. It hurt Kilo and Louve to have to leave him in there, but they were glad that he had made it and was thriving. Kore was so small, weighing only three pounds when born and finally putting on enough weight, but his lungs needed to develop more. They were for sure he would have asthma and a few other issues, but overall will live a full life like any other child.

Mama Loucille was driving like a bat out of hell as she headed to the strip club on two wheels. I have no clue why Louve let her ass drive, but I guess it may be since Louve had drunk a whole bottle of Stella Rosa Black by herself. I was nervous as hell, but after Loucille saw the Snapchats that Big Ed had made, she was on ten and out for blood. They had just renewed their vows, and Edge and I were set to marry in a small ceremony tomorrow and have the big wedding after the

baby was born. I guess the men called themselves having a
bachelor party, and since me and the ladies were blocked for
our men's pages, Big Ed was the only one who got caught slip-
ping probably because he didn't know how to work the damn
apps.

"Ma, can you slow down, please? We would like to make it
there and not crash, please." Louve said, holding the handle
above her head as we pulled into the parking lot of the strip
club.

"We here now, so hush girl and come on because your
daddy got me fucked to the all the way up okurrrrttt," she
said doing a bad impersonation of Cardi B.

"I'm with you Mama Lou because Dreon Alves clearly has
lost his damn mind if he thinks I'm going to be home
carrying around his damn baby while he out at strip clubs
with dusty ass strippers in his lap. Oh hell no, I don't think
so!" Egypt yelled, waddling her all belly self around the car
and storming into the club.

Now even though we only stepped out to pull our men
out, we still came dressed to kill it. I was still sporting my
heels in a bandage dress with my fresh blown out bob parted
down the middle. My makeup was beat, and my brows were
popping. I did an once-over, and we were all looking good as
hell. Louve had her snapback figure. As always after each
child, she snaps right the hell back damn near instantly. She
was dressed in a fitted pair of high waist Fashion Nova jeans
and a black crop top off the shoulder shirt with some black
heels. Her face was natural with just gloss, and her hair was
pulled up in a high ponytail with some shiny ass diamonds in
her ears. Egypt wore a long fitted maxi dress with a split up
one thigh and a pair of peep toe chunky booties.

Mama Loucille fitted right in with her flat stomach and
thick body she had picked up over the months being home
and clean. She had that happy love weight on her, and it

looked damn good. Mama Loucille wore a halter one-piece fitted pants romper with some nude pumps and a matching bag. Her natural hair was slick back into a bun, and she didn't look a day over 40 but was in her 50s.

As soon as we approached the door, Aunt Vera was pulling Uncle Vern out the door by his ear, and he was sloppy drunk trying to slap her ass and laughing.

We didn't even stop. She waved and kept going so we stepped in where the strippers were going in for the twerking contest. I scanned the room and found the men in the biggest VIP section with strippers everywhere around them. I tried to pull Louve to the side to warn her of the show her daddy was receiving, but it was too late. Mama Loucille was marching in that direction as we hurried and tried to catch up to her. Big Ed had a stripper's ass twerking all in his face, and he was just slapping ass and making it rain. I was trying not to laugh but to see him posted up in VIP like he wasn't a whole grandpa out here was beyond hilarious.

Edge looked like the spitting image of his father, so I understood why Mama Loucille was on ten because he was a handsome older man, and he was definitely gone have young and older bitches on him now that he was a free man. Mama Lou reached the men just as the stripper laid on her back and cocked her legs wide open, thrusting her pelvis up and down on a table in front of Big Ed. That poor girl ain't know what the hell was happening as Mama Loucille tossed her ass over a rail and slap the shit out of Big Ed.

He was stunned at first, but he jumped up, threw Mama Loucille over his shoulder, and carried her ass out the VIP and out the door. Edge was on me before I could even be on him about the hoes up in his section. I smelled his cologne before he even was in my space fully.

"Why is my pregnant wife in a strip club full of smoke and

shit? That ain't good for my baby boy?" he said, kissing my
neck.

"I'm a laugh when this is a damn girl. And your soon to be
wife is in here to get her man who seems to think he can be
out here acting like a single ass man," I replied.

We kissed and were damn near ready get shit popping in
the section until the commotion caused us to break our
kissing and head over to what was going on.

"Let me tell yo thirsty ass something, bitch. I let your
lies stir up some shit the last time, but I know for a fact my
man ain't even look your way with that linty ass lingerie set
on. Bitch, your broke ass is still out trying to get our men.
You better ask around because the wives of these real Hittas
ain't no joke!" Egypt yelled in Kelli's face. Kelli was just
looking stupid as she tried to grab all her ones up and scurry
away.

Drip finally got Egypt to walk down the stairs so that we
could all leave. Even though the guys were no longer worried
about anyone being after them, they had kept JP and the
others on the payroll. JP escorted us all out the trucks that
waited for us. We all got in one individually and headed home
with our men. I didn't want to break the tradition of not
seeing your man the morning of the wedding, so when we got
to the house, I let Edge know I was going to stay at Kilo and
Louve's house.

"Man, fuck that. I need my wife in the bed with me
tonight. Look at this shit, Tori. We need you home," he
replied, placing my hand on his thigh where his anaconda was
stretched along the length of his thigh. He knew my weak-
ness and how to get my ass.

"This is why I'm pregnant now out of wedlock because of
you and him," I said, squeezing it lightly.

"That shit doesn't matter if it's out of wedlock, man. You
and my son are my world, and we're a family. Y'all come first

before anything and anyone, remember that shit, T," Edge said, kissing me deeply.

He opened the door to the truck, stepped out, and then helped me out. We didn't even make it past the living room before he had me bent over sliding up in me. He was becoming addicted to my honey pot now that I was pregnant.

"Damn Tori, this shit is so damn wet and gushy. I'm going to have to keep you pregnant fuckkkk! You already had some good ass shit that had me in deep, but this shit is off the fucking charts, ma. I love you, Tori. Tell me you love me." He was talking all this while sliding in out of my center, hitting my spot with each thrust.

"OHHH, yes! EDGE, I LOVE YOU!" I moaned out.

————

We stood hand in hand in front of the ordained minister ready to tie the knot. We snuck off just us early this morning to make it official. The family was going to kick our asses, but this was about us and our love for each other, not them. Seeing the tears sitting on the brim of Edge's eyelids was confirmation that this was right. I loved him beyond his crazy ways and tactics, and he has loved me since the day we decided to explore into that territory of love. I could probably find a man that would love me flaws and all, but there was only one Edge, and I was gone be here with until the end of time.

"I now pronounce you man and wife," the minister stated.

I kissed my husband, and I felt like I was floating on a cloud. I was now, Mrs. Tori Luxe. I was over the top and extra, but surprisingly, this simple ceremony was satisfying. Now, I won't act as if I don't have an extra ass wedding in the works because I damn sure do, but it'll be after we welcome our bundle of joy.

Edge led me out to the car, and we headed back to the house as husband and wife. The ride with this man ain't been easy, but I was completely happy and in love, and as long as he continues to do right by me, I was with him for the long haul.

Chapter Twenty-Four

KILO

I laid back in the bed just reflecting on life as Louve slept on my chest. We had gone at it all night, but I couldn't sleep. I was feeling like the luckiest nigga in the world. I had married the woman of my dreams, and after all the bullshit, she was here rocking with me. I had four beautiful children, and I was building a relationship with my parents. Ms. Lolly, who I now had started to call Grams, was a godsend. She came in, brought so much to our lives, and was the sweetest woman any kid could want as a grandmother, and I was thankful my kids had her. I was ready to bring Kore home, and the doctors had already set the date for two weeks from now.

We had everything ready for him to come home, and I knew Louve would be happy as hell. She beat herself up for a while about the whole situation, and she was finally starting to live and be somewhat happy. She felt terrible being out of the hospital without Kore and thought she wasn't allowed to live. I shut that down quickly and let her know it didn't make her less of a woman or mother. Just thinking of the lengths she has gone for us made me proud to have her.

I kissed her forehead and smoked on my blunt while

staring at her curves as the night sky shone in through the blinds on her body. Louve was perfect in every way to me, and I was honored to have made her my wife. She carried both my last names proudly with me. I decided that I wanted to keep my mother and father's last names since they never officially married. I was a Denton on paper, but for most of my life, my mother said my last name was Jones. I just put Denton in between, and Louve did the same the day we went to the courthouse.

Money was no longer a problem for us, and my family would never struggle again a day in their life. I provided the way I felt was necessary as the man of the house. I was hustling on a scale way larger than I could have ever imagined. Drip, Edge, and I had the grand opening of the club coming up in a few days, and I was excited as hell to have that spot open. The restaurant was doing big things and with Ms. Lolly, Drip's grandma Ms. Alves, and the help of my in-laws along with Uncle Vern and Aunt Vera, shit was good for us all. Looking back, I never thought we would have elevated this quickly through the game and be running our own businesses as well. Shit was mind-blowing and a dope ass feeling.

———

I was up and out of the house early because I had to handle some business for the grand opening and decided to slide by Drip's new house. Grand Luxe Lounge was going to be a dope upscale club for our people to have a good time with good music, drinks, and entertainment. The hiring process took the longest, and now we just were awaiting the delivery of the furniture and lighting fixtures. We had the city buzzing about the grand opening. Louve wasn't feeling the attention because she had her concerns about how things went down when I first started seeing money a while back. I assured her that I'd be on my best behavior. I learned my lessons, and I had a second chance with my family, and that was all that mattered in life to me.

I pulled up to Drip and Egypt's newly built home, and I was proud of my bro. This house was dope as hell, and they land for days. I pulled in the long ass driveway, and I hopped out. I rang the bell, and it swung open quickly, and Drip stood there like he saw a ghost.

"Bro drive us to the hospital Egypt water just broke," Drip said, turning around to go get a screaming Egypt.

"Oh shit, hurry up bro, I'm a start the car," I took off to the car and started it up. I shot all the family a text message to meet us at the hospital.

Drip came to the door helping Egypt out. I was so damn confused because I know she wasn't due yet, but she damn sure looked like it. Louve got big, but nothing like this. It looked as if she had more than one damn baby in there. I was so engrossed in staring at her huge protruding belly that I didn't hop out to help them in my truck. Snapping out of my trance, I hopped out as Drip placed Egypt in the back, and I grabbed the bags he had sat by the door and put them in the trunk. We hopped back in, and I sped out the driveway in reverse almost knocking the mailbox over.

"DREONNNN, baby, this hurts! I can't do thisssss!" Egypt yelled out in agony.

I looked at Drip, and he looked at me like he was scared too. He climbed from the front to back and cradled Egypt as I drove as fast as I could to get them there. From the way she was carrying on, I'd guess that her labor was in full swing. I was burning rubber to get them there fast and no sooner than I knew it, we were pulling up to the ER entrance.

Drip hopped out and went to help Egypt while I went around to the front to alert staff of her labor. The nurses, doctors, and other staff members all rushed to help her inside. Drip went back with them, and I parked the car and made my way back to the ER waiting room. Once seated, I dialed Louve, and she told me she was on her way down to the ER now from the NICU. She went to see Kore first, and I then remembered we'd all be taking a baby home in a matter of days. Louve made it down and sat with me, and no sooner than that, everyone made their way into the waiting area to wait.

Chapter Twenty-Five

DRIP

Everything happened so fast that I felt like I was in the twilight zone. Egypt was laid on her side, and I was slow stroking her for the third time this day, and that last time we obviously caused some issues. She started complaining of pains and then she got up to pee, and her water broke. I was scared because we were a couple of weeks shy of eight months and the baby was coming already. I was nervous as hell as the doctor's hooked up Egypt to all these monitors and shit.

"Why does she need oxygen? Is my wife ok?" I asked as they hurried around me, ignoring my questions.

"Mr. Alves, trust us. Your wife is in good hands, and we are giving her oxygen as a precaution. There's no cause for alarm," a nurse finally stopped and said to me before going back to hooking Egypt's IV up.

Today was the day my life would forever change. I was about to have a child, and I was on top of the world about that. I called my grandma, and she said she was already in the car with Ms. Lolly and would be here soon. Egypt was in a lot of pain, and I was hurt as fuck that I couldn't help ease it for her. I was finally able to come close to her bed and hold her hands and provide her some comfort through the pain.

"I WANT MY TUBES TIED NOW!" Egypt screamed aloud squeezing my hand tight.

I just kissed her forehead and tried to calm her down. No sooner than I did that, the doctor waltz in did a check on her and said she was ready to push. I got ready right with the doctor, and we counted down for Egypt to push. She was pushing hard, and I took a peek around her legs where the doctor was, and it was the worst but most beautiful sight I ever saw. I could see a head full of curly hair, and this shit gave me goosebumps all over. The baby that I helped to create was in on the way, but I also couldn't believe how wide my honey pot was. I hope that shit shrinks back but not get all shriveled up like roast beef.

The sound of cries snapped me out my trance, and a nurse shoved the scissors in my hand, and I clipped the umbilical cord. They placed the baby on top of Egypt, and she cried and kissed her.

"I feel like I have to push some more, I think I have to poop," Egypt said, looking embarrassed.

"No, my dear that's the other baby it's crowning," the doctor said, taking my baby girl from us, and passing her to the nurse quickly.

"WHAT THE HELL ARE YOU TALKING ABOUT? OHHH, SHIT! THIS HURTS. DRIP, WHAT IS GOING ON?" Egypt was having a full panic attack and was in tears.

I had no response. I was in shock and couldn't even make sense of anything. The doctor told me to hold her leg while the nurse went around to the other side, and we counted again, and Egypt pushed. One push and another baby came right out, smaller than the first, but a loud, strong cry followed. I had tears in my eyes, and I was feeling blessed. I went to cut the cord again, and Egypt was in position ready to push again, and I was confused. What the hell is going on?

"This is insane. It's another head crowning," was all I heard before I blacked out.

———

I woke up with people over me calling my name. The room was bright, and my head was banging. I slowly sat up and then was helped up off the ground by the nurses and staff around me. My eyes locked with Egypt, and she was holding three small babies on her chest, and she had this glow that radiating through the room. I walked over to the bed and looked down in amazement at what we were blessed with. It was a miracle that we had triplets. The doctor told us the two smallest babies were hidden behind the biggest one but had developed perfectly, and for multiples, they came on time and not too early like we were worried about.

I came in a nervous wreck about having my first child, and I just had three the first go around. I was quickly on board with E for them tubes to be tied. I had two girls and a boy. Our youngest and smallest of the bunch was our baby boy, my Jr. Dreon A.K.A DJ, weighed four pounds even. The oldest of the trio was Emory Drae. She weighed four pounds eight ounces. The middle child was Emoni Drae, who weighed four pounds five ounces. We had delivered a healthy set of triplets, and I had to announce to the family the shocking but great news. I kissed Egypt and my babies and headed to the door.

"I love Mrs. Alves, and Thank you," I said as I stared at her from the doorway.

"I love you too, Dreon. Thank you for what?" she asked with a confused and sleepy look.

"For giving me a second chance and those miracles of ours

that you are holding. I am forever indebted to you. You gave me a purpose, and this family of ours means everything to me. A nigga never felt more solid and complete than I do this very moment, ma," I replied with all sincerity. I just wanted her to know how much she and our kids mean to me.

The meds were setting in, and I could see from the high look on E's face she was heading to sleep. The nurses took the babies and placed them in the rolling cribs, and off to the nursery they went.

EPILOGUE

Louve

The kids played with baby Kore all over the house now that he was officially walking. I folded up the laundry and had a flashback from a year ago about the way my life got flipped upside down. I had moved past that and was the happiest I had ever been in my life. I came from my thoughts and smiled at Kore as he walked around like Frankenstein as he followed his sisters through the house. KJ was so happy to have a brother, and the girls were taking their big sister role serious. They all helped me daily, and it was the cutest thing. Kore was still so little to me, but despite how early he came, he beat all the odds and was making strides. His first birthday had just passed, and after all the months he spent in the hospital, he was healthy and active. We were all obsessed with him.

Tori and Edge's Big wedding was this weekend, and I couldn't wait for the big day. We were already bonded, and this just solidified it for us once and for all. Family was so important to me, and even though mines had taken through hell and back, they were most important to me. I had four beautiful children and a husband that loved me and catered to me. My mother was clean, and my father was home raising hell and being him. My kids had a full family, and with all the new babies, it had grown so big.

Kilo had been building a bond with his mother and trying to get to know his father despite the mental issues. Mama Jones would be released in a few months after her case was tossed out on a technicality. We asked no questions. We just thanked God and kept living in the blessings. Kilo hired the best lawyers for his mom, and the best doctors to help his father get better. I saw a light in Kilo I never saw before, and it made me so happy to see that. Kilo wasn't perfect by far, but he was doing everything necessary to repair us, and so far, he'd done above and beyond.

We had finally branched off into real estate, and we owned a few homes that we rented out. We had the lounge and the restaurant as well, and things were going so well for us all involved. I still had my plans for myself and the things I wanted, but I was happy raising my family at the moment. We purchased a home for Kilo's mother around the corner from us on the same block as my parents' new home. Drip had finally convinced his grandmother to move out the hood, and he purchased her a bungalow on the same street as well. After Muse passed, Grandma Alves was finally ready to leave the hood.

Ms. Lolly wasn't too far, either living in the senior community that she loved. She and Ms. Alves had become thick as thieves and were now bingo buddies. They had all these grandbabies to love on and keep us all grounded and in line as well. Without Ms. Lolly, I may have never given Kilo a chance to make things right, but she got me all the way together, and here we were. Mrs. Alves was usually home and doing her own thing, but now that she is closer to us all we get the talks and wisdom from her too.

Poor Drip was stressed the hell out with the three babies

and Egypt, but he took that shit and handled it like a man was supposed to. When Drip came out and told us that they had just given birth to triplets, we all were in complete shock. It made sense though because Egypt was freakishly huge, and we all kept our mouths shut, so we didn't get cursed out by her, but she definitely was way bigger than she should have been for one damn baby, so yea, that made perfect damn sense. Emory, Emoni, and DJ were so cute and adorable that it had me ready to have a few more, but after the things I have gone through with pregnancies and hard labors, I think Kore is the last one. Egypt wasn't playing. She had the IUD put in ASAP because the pills were tampered with before thanks to Drip so this way, he couldn't sneak three damn babies on her again.

Drip swear they gone have one more to even it out, and he swears it's gone be a boy, but Egypt is terrified they will be that couple who has multiples each time. Four was perfect for us, and we were done with that. Edge is lucky to have got his one in with Tori because that girl was not hearing that shit about a baby, but they had just welcomed their son named East. They chose not to find out the gender until the baby was born, and just like Edge predicted, it was a boy. Tori had the perfect pregnancy and did all those first-time mom things. She had an underwater maternity shoot, a cast done of her belly, and planned the biggest baby shower. Even with the wedding approaching, she still made sure her pregnancy was a great experience. Let Tori tell it, and they were one and done, but I doubt Edge would go for that.

My brother was obsessed with his nephew and never wanted to let us love him. I went over there yesterday, and at three months East has more shit than all my kids combined. I tried to hold him, but Edge couldn't let him out his sight. It was so cute seeing them fight over the baby. Tori wants to not spoil East so that she can go back to school and work, but

Edge has already spoiled that boy rotten. East could whine, and Edge comes flying to him, and all I can do is crack up.

Edge damn near cursed us out for taking so long to make his baby boy's bottle. We were literally in the kitchen for a few minutes, and East cried too long for Edge, so he came in that kitchen, snatched that bottle from Tori, and said we were too busy gossiping and had his son starving. I fell out in tears, and Tori damn near cursed me out because of it. I feel bad for my sis. She's got to deal with my crazy ass brother and his mini-me in training.

I look back on all the craziness and can't believe how we came out on top. We never expected everything to come full circle as it had but look at us now. This family has weathered many storms, many secrets, and the lies had almost torn us apart, but we stuck through and stood strong together. Each test we got through, and although it wasn't easy and many time, we all folded or tried to let go somehow, we pushed through to get to the best part. They say it gets greater later and I truly believe that.

Chapter Twenty-Six

EDGE

Today was the day I would marry Tori in front of everyone. We had made things official at the courthouse a long time ago, but she deserved the wedding of her dreams. I had my father as my best man, and my boys Drip and Kilo as my groomsmen. My nephews and nieces were in the wedding too. I was finally a father and East was perfect. My son had my heart right along with his mama. I kept East with me all night while the ladies went out for drinks and a good time. It was all good because over the years I had my share of fun, and I didn't need my mama rounding the crew up and busting up in the strip club like they did before.

Ms. Lolly and Mama Alves were coming to gather all the kids and get them ready for the ceremony, so I gathered up East's diaper bag and the mini garment bag with his baby tux. Once the kids were all rounded up, I proceeded to get ready for the wedding. I had less than two hours to get from the house to the Ritz Carlton where the wedding and reception were being held. I had emotions the day of our wedding at the justice of the peace, but I wondered what I'd feel when I saw my woman in her dress coming down the aisle to me.

The time flew by, and I was out the door and in the truck, while JP drove me to the Ritz. When we pulled up the guest were lined up awaiting entry, and I spotted Drip, my father and Kilo making their way inside. I hopped out and jogged over to them to catch up. Once we entered the lobby, my Aunt Vera was on us like white on rice to get our boutonnieres pinned to our tux and get pictures taken. I did as I was told and then took my place at the altar made from flowers. The set up was dope and looked like something from off a TV show for weddings.

The guys lined up with me, and we anticipated the ceremony beginning. I kept looking at my watch, realizing that in a matter of minutes, my wife would be walking in to marry me again in front of everyone. The attendees filed in and filled the rows of seats in. I looked at my baby boy dressed in the same version of my tux in baby form as Ms. Lolly fed him a bottle. I checked my Rolex and realized that we were a few minutes after show time and the doors had yet to open and the music hadn't begun. Tori was prompt and never late and especially not for her wedding day, so these few minutes behind schedule had me wondering what the hell was going on.

I wouldn't panic though I'd keep my cool and give her some time maybe the traffic of something with her hair or makeup was to blame. I smiled at everyone and looked to the guys, and they looked cool, so I kept my cool. The minister came in and took his place, shaking my hand as he got his things ready and in place. I rechecked my watch, and the time had jumped to minutes behind schedule. I looked to Mama Alves and pointed at my watch. She shrugged her shoulders and leaned over to Ms. Lolly, who was seated beside her and whispered something.

Mama Alves got up and headed out of the room we were in for the ceremony. Ms. Lolly smiled still feeding East and mouthed to me not to worry. That was easier said than done at this point. Mama Alves came back in smiling wide, and the music began to play. My heart warmed as the doors opened, and I watched my nephews KJ and Kore walk down holding hands and a pillow in each hand. We had to find the small pillow that snapped around Kore's wrist so that he wouldn't drop it.

They reached us, and Mama Alves made it up front in time to meet them at the end of the aisle so that she could sit them down beside her. I looked to the door as the staff rolled down the runner. Once the runner was down, my nieces came out looking like the two little princesses they were. They dropped the flowers from their baskets and came to the end and then went to sit where their brothers were. Behind them was Drip and Egypt's nanny with the triplets. Between my family and Tori's plus our friends and associates, the room was packed to capacity. Tori's pops had passed when she was young, and her mother left after all her kids were grown to run off with her new rich white husband, so she opted to have my Uncle Vern walk her down the aisle.

The doors reopened, and there she was looking like a queen. Tori's stomach snapped back after East was born, so her body was still on point. She had filled out in hips, but it looked good as hell on her. She came down the aisle with her veil on as the music played.

"I found love in you
And I've learned to love me too
Never have I felt that I could be all that you see
It's like our hearts have intertwined into the perfect harmony
This is why I love you
Ooh this is why I love you
Because you love me
You love me
This is why I love you

Ooh this is why I love you
Because you love me
You love me."

I listened as the song we chose played, and a nigga's eyes were sweating like hell. I wiped the tears, and I knew this woman was my world. I never felt the way I did about any of the other females in my life like I feel about Tori. We had the perfect son, and she loved me beyond my fucked-up ways and flaws. I have become better as a man and a person because of her. Uncle Vern handed her hand to me, and I took it and kissed it. I lifted her veil, and we stared at each other intensely.

I was present but only for her. I heard the reverend and followed all his directions, but it was all muffled and blurred around me. I had tunnel vision on my beautiful wife in front of me. By the time I tuned back in fully, it was now time to kiss my bride, and I gladly did that. I kissed her and picked her up in my arms. I'd married her over a thousand times because we were in this shit forever. I did some crazy things, she played back the way I played, and that shit set my ass straight. Forever and a day I was rocking with Tori the long way.

———

Our reception was lit and turned all the way up. I was at the bar throwing back shots with my father and then Kilo. I watched as the ladies tore the floor up twerking and acting out. My family was having the time of their lives, and we all deserved it. The restaurant was doing damn good and stayed packed. The lounge was doing beyond what we expected, and we had opted to open another one in Atlanta. Our business with the Dons was still operating smoothly, and we had money coming in left and right on the daily.

We made our way to the dance floor with the ladies, and I was glad to see everyone together and happy. I was able to allow my parents just to be grandparents, travel and live life, and they were doing just that. Having them back in the picture was major for us, and they brought balance to us all. They accepted Tori with open arms and Kilo as well. Louve and I had finally repaired our relationship, and life was in its prime. Looking around the room again, I took a moment to thank God. I wasn't a saint or religious in the least bit, but after witnessing the things I had, I knew we were all blessed to be in this moment.

The End

L. RENEE'S CATALOG

CPSIA information can be obtained
at www.ICGtesting.com
Printed in the USA
LVHW091607130919
631008LV00002B/181/P

9 781691 314423